I0687790

Greetings from Avondale

Mistletoe MISTAKE

USA TODAY BESTSELLING AUTHOR
AMALI ROSE

Mistletoe Mistake
Copyright © 2020 by Amali Rose

This book is a work of fiction. Names and characters, places, and incidents are the product of the author's imagination or are used fictitiously. Any resemblance to actual events, locales, or persons, living or dead, is coincidental.

Editing: Ellie McLove - My Brother's Editor
Proofreading: Rosa Sharon - My Brother's Editor
Cover Design: Ben Ellis – Tall Story Design

All rights reserved. In accordance with the U.S. Copyright Act of 1976, electronic sharing of any part of this book without the permission of the publisher or author constitute unlawful piracy and theft of the author's intellectual property. If you would like to use the material from this book (other than for review purposes), prior written permission must be obtained by contacting the publisher at authoramalirose@gmail.com. Thank you for your support of the author's rights.

FBI Anti-Piracy Warning:

The unauthorized reproduction or distribution of a copyrighted work is illegal. Criminal copyright infringement, including infringement without monetary gain, is investigated by the FBI, and is punishable by up to five years in prison, and a fine of $250,000.

Mistletoe MISTAKE

This book is for Gypsy.
You came into my life on Christmas Day 2004 and stole my heart.
You made every single day better and I miss you as fiercely as I love you.

"Christmas isn't just a day, it's a frame of mind."
Valentine Davies (Miracle on 34th Street)

SYNOPSIS

I hate Christmas.

Before you scream bah humbug, let me explain: my
birthday is December 25th.

Birthdays were largely ignored, and the holiday lost its
luster before I hit double digits. I didn't get a birthday
party—instead, my parents spent their energy planning
a huge Christmas party.

So when the annual Christmas party rolls around
again, it's nothing more than an obligation to endure.

Until this year. Because this year, Nick O'Connor will
be there. Bad boy extraordinaire. Brutally beautiful,
he's the strong and silent type. Also, my brother's best
friend.

When he finds me under the mistletoe, he might just
convince me to fall in love with Christmas after all.

And him too, while I'm at it.

HOLLY

"*H*ow do I look?"

I take a step back, narrow my eyes and sweep an appraising look along my friend's body. I want to say something nice, truly I do. In an effort to buy some time, I scan my office, letting my attention fall on the small bookshelf that holds my *Friends* Funko Pop! collection. I stare hard at '80s Chandler, as though he will somehow help me come up with a *nice* way to say what I'm thinking. Although on second thought, Chandler might not be the best character to find inspiration in.

I sigh and decide it's a hopeless cause, I put on my big girl panties and turn back to Troy.

"You know those scary Santa pictures from the '70s and '80s that do the rounds on Facebook every year?"

His face pinches in an entirely unflattering expression as he nods.

"You look like that."

Troy snatches the Santa hat off his head and throws it at me with all the aggression of a cuddly teddy bear. Which is to say, none.

"You're a bitch, Hols." He flops down onto the tiny sofa I have squeezed into my equally tiny office.

Stifling a laugh, I take a seat next to him and rest my head on his shoulder.

"What were you thinking when you volunteered to be Santa?"

His sigh fills the room. "I was thinking that if I didn't, there would be no Santa at Tahlia's kindergarten Christmas party."

I wrinkle my nose in distaste which draws a chuckle from Troy.

"Most normal people would see that as a bad thing."

"Christmas is overrated, I've explained this to you so many times." I give his bicep a squeeze and shift on the sofa so that I am facing him.

"Five-year-olds don't care about your childhood trauma, Holly. In fact, me volunteering to do *this*." He motions to the bright red suit he's wearing. "Is meant to stop Tahlia from experiencing her own trauma."

He shifts awkwardly, and I really do feel awful for him. Since the moment his daughter was born, she has been Troy and Matthew's entire world. Now, at the ripe old age of five, she has her dads wrapped around her little finger. As evidenced by jolly St. Nicholas in front of me.

"You're a good dad. Unfortunately, I think if you turn up looking like that you're going to have the opposite effect."

"Then help me." Troy groans and pushes himself up to stand in front of me. Hands on hips and his brow furrowed, I can practically smell the desperation on him.

"Okay, first things first. This" —I wave a finger at the Santa suit that looks like it was made in the same decade as those scary Santa pictures— "is ancient. Stop being such a cheapskate and spend the money to rent a decent suit." I take a minute to observe the way his mouth twitches and how he swallows hard at my advice.

"Fine. Anything else?" His tone is decidedly grumpier than it was a moment ago, and I bite my lip to hide a smile. Troy's infamous for his miserly ways, and I know the thought of spending money will be killing him.

"You need to get some padding." I eye his lanky frame critically. "You're way too skinny to pull Santa off without it."

"Jesus Christ," he mutters, yanking off the suit jacket.

"Yeah, also, maybe cut out the JC cursing. It's not very Christmassy." I smile sweetly at him.

"Bite m—"

"Knock knock," he's cut off by my roommate, Billie, who is standing at my office door. "Holly, I've got your —" Her eyes widen when she notices Troy standing there in Santa pants and a dress shirt, his short blond hair mussed, and she bursts out laughing.

"You both suck." He storms toward the door and

brushes past Billie, muttering about getting back to work.

"Is that my straightener?"

"Yeah." She steps into my office and hands it to me. "How long are you house-sitting for your brother? The apartment is quiet without you and Gypsy. No loud music playing and no dog howling along to your terrible singing." She smirks and follows me as I move to my desk, taking a seat opposite me. I sink down on my desk chair and feel the familiar ache in my back. I really need to check out that ergonomic desk chair my chiropractor was telling me about.

"You missing us already? We only left yesterday."

"Did I say anything about missing you? I said it was quiet. I *like* the quiet." She raises an eyebrow at me and I roll my eyes. It will be a cold day in hell before she admits to anything as sentimental as feelings.

"You're an ass. But thank you for bringing me this." I tap the tongs and then give my wavy brown locks a tug. "My hair is a nightmare without it."

"Not a problem." She shrugs. "So, how long?"

"Just a week. Brandon and Amy get back on the twenty-third." I pull a face. "They couldn't miss the Christmas party."

"Speaking of which, your dad asked me to tell you that he got your email about the party and he regrets to inform you that boycotting Christmas is not a valid reason to miss it this year." She shakes her head at me and a strand of fiery red hair escapes her low bun. "Just like it wasn't last year. Or the year before that."

I scrunch up a Post-it note and throw it at her. "I thought you were here as my roommate, not as Dad's assistant."

"I hate to break it to you, but we are one and the same. I'll let him know that you'll be there and you couldn't be more excited." She stands up and stretches before heading out.

"He'll never believe that," I call out behind her. Her only response is to flip me the bird.

I laugh lightly and turn back to my computer, trying to remember where I was with the birthday card design I was working on before Troy interrupted me.

Before I can get back to work, my phone rings. Noting it's the internal line, I answer with my attention still mostly on the design in front of me.

"Holly, sweetheart." My dad's voice booms down the line.

"What's up, Dad?"

"Your brother's trying to get in touch with you, but he said your phone keeps going to voicemail."

I groan and grab my cell phone out of the desk drawer, only to discover it's completely dead. "I forgot to charge it last night. Did he say what he wanted?"

"No, just that he wants you to call him."

"Okay, was that all?"

"Your email was very entertaining," he replies dryly, and a small grin plays on my lips.

"Why thank you, I try my best." I giggle.

"You know, you'll have to get over this Christmas hatred thing eventually."

"That's not going to happen. Christmas sealed its fate on my tenth birthday when no one turned up to my party because they were suffering from post-Christmas exhaustion. I was ten, Dad. Ten! Then there was the yea—"

"I remember it all, sweetie," he cuts me off mid-rant. "But Christmas is such a wonderful time of the year. It's about love and family and everything that's important." His voice softens, gaining the sentimental tone he gets when discussing any holiday.

My father is unapologetically emotional about special occasions. It's one of the things that led him to opening a greeting card company with my mother so many years ago and, while I would never say this to his face, his sentimentality has only gotten worse with age.

"I know, I know," I sigh, tiredly. We have this same argument year after year. But seriously, if your birthday was December twenty-fifth, you would resent sharing your special day too.

"I have to go, Dad, I'm in the middle of a project, but I'll talk to you later, okay?"

He relents and we say our goodbyes.

It's moments like this that I don't entirely love working at *Greetings from Avondale*. Originally a small boutique greeting card company, my parents started the business before my brother was born. It has grown and expanded over the years and is now one of the most successful greeting card companies in the US.

I always loved coming here as a child. It felt like a second home to me and when I graduated with a degree in graphic design three years ago, it was only natural I start working for the company that was such an intrinsic part of my family.

Plus, despite how I feel about Christmas, I did inherit my father's love of holidays and special occasions, and there is something almost magical about creating a keepsake for people to celebrate the most important moments in their lives.

I may hate Christmas, but I love my job.

§.

"C'mon." I jiggle the key in the lock and mentally cross my fingers that it will work this time. Brandon warned me that this lock was sticking. He promised he would fix it before they left, but I guess he didn't get around to it. Ugh, which reminds me, I never called my brother to see what he wanted. I sigh, hating how the day got away from me. I can hear Gypsy on the other side of the door, sniffing around and scratching at the door to get to me. Finally, with one last jiggle and a silent prayer, the key turns and the door swings open. I trek through the mudroom, into the kitchen and dump my things on the island counter, before crouching down and greeting my fur baby with ear scratches and a tummy rub. When she's suitably loved up, she gives me a final lick and races off to her toys where she busies herself with a tennis ball.

Groaning, I roll my shoulders and slump onto the counter, considering what to do for dinner. Deciding that a grilled cheese will have to do, I'm halfway to the refrigerator when I remember the spa bath Brandon and Amy had installed in their bathroom earlier this year and suddenly my plans for the night change. I grab a glass and a bottle of wine—*Moscato, my favorite, thank you Amy*—from the refrigerator and I head toward the stairs, already fantasizing about sinking into a tub full of bubbles.

I've barely made it three steps when my newly charged phone starts buzzing in my purse. I groan and try to decide whether or not to ignore it. Guilt stops me, knowing Brandon will most likely be annoyed he's been chasing me all day, so I turn back to the counter and search through my bag until I find it. Unexpectedly seeing my friend Tessa's name on the screen, I answer the call and greet her warmly. After a few minutes of small talk, I grab the wine with my spare hand, and pivot back in the direction of the stairs, figuring I'll switch to speaker and finish the conversation while I get my bath ready.

"Anyway, I'm calling about book club." Tessa's usually melodic voice sounds worried.

"What's up?" I take the stairs two at a time, eager to reach paradise. I can already feel the tension start to leave my body, imagining my body sinking into the hot water.

"I know we were supposed to have our next meeting at my apartment, but I've had a business trip sprung on me, so I'm going to be out of state until the twenty-third."

My feet hit the landing and I turn toward the bathroom.

"Oh, that's no problem, Tess. Billie and I can host it this time and you can FaceTime us."

"You're sure?"

"Of course." I reach for the bathroom door and open it, already planning the night in my head. "Our place is p—p—penis!"

2

NICK

I should probably cover my dick.

She hasn't taken her bright blue eyes off it since she flung open the bathroom door, and that was at least thirty seconds ago.

Thirty long, *silent* seconds ago.

The little fucker seems to be getting off on her attention though, because it twitches, and her round eyes get even wider.

Yeah, I really should cover my dick.

"Hey, Holly." I continue to scrub the towel over my hair.

My voice seems to startle her, and I wish I could adequately describe the sound she makes. Imagine a strangled screech, some garbled words and a deep exhalation of breath. Now imagine all three mixed together, and you might come close to the sound I just experienced.

I'm not going to lie, my cock has never gotten a reaction like that before and I'm not mad about it.

Taking pity on her, I lazily wrap the towel around my waist and turn to face her, scratching my pec as I do. A sparking sensation under my skin follows the path of her eyes and I realize I might be in trouble.

"Sorry, I should have locked the door. I was filthy and in a rush to clean up. I wasn't thinking." My apology is half-assed because I can't count the number of times I've imagined her eyes on me like this.

A small squeak escapes her full, pink mouth, reminding me of a cartoon character, and she abruptly turns, making her escape back the way she came.

Well, that could have gone better.

Ten minutes later I walk into the kitchen to find Holly pacing back and forth, her arms wrapped firmly around her waist and her bottom lip clamped between her teeth.

I would also like to point out that I am now fully dressed. Winning at life, right here.

"You okay?"

She startles at the sound of my voice before turning to face me. The scorching sensation under my skin fires back to life.

This is definitely going to be a problem.

"Yeah." She smiles ruefully. "Sorry about that, I didn't realize you were here."

"I guess Brandon didn't tell you he said I could stay for a few days?" I make a mental note to kick my best friend's ass.

Something akin to understanding lights up her eyes. "He was trying to call me today, but we didn't connect." She shakes her head and mutters something under her breath that I don't quite catch.

"Ah, well, there's some plumbing problems at my apartment and I needed a place to stay for a couple of days. Brandon said it would be okay for me to crash here." I grimace before continuing. "I hope that's okay? I can always find a hotel…"

"Of course it's fine! Um, I guess we don't both need to be here though." Her brows pull together and a cute little line appears. "I can go back to my apartment until you're gone." She gives her head a little nod, as if it's decided.

Fuck no.

"Don't do that." Shit, that might have come out slightly more aggressive than I meant it to, because her head instantly pops up, looking at me with surprise written all over her face. "I just mean, I'm only going to be here a couple of days. You'll only just finish unpacking and it'll be time for you to come back. You might as well stay."

"I guess that's true." She nibbles her lip. "All right, I guess being roomies for a couple of days won't kill me." Moving toward the island, she takes a seat on one of the uncomfortable-looking stools. "Have you eaten? I'm starving."

A bark sounds from the mudroom and her little dog comes rushing out and drops a ball at my feet.

"I can always eat." I bend down and scoop up the furball who starts wriggling in my arms and trying to lick my face. "She's not much of a guard dog, you know." I sit on the stool next to her—FYI, they're just as uncomfortable as they look—still trying to wrangle the brown and white dog. "When I got here, all she did was sniff me and claw my legs until I picked her up."

Her face softens as she watches Gypsy, who has turned her attention to Holly and is trying to jump from my arms to hers.

"Yeah, the only way she'll ever stop an intruder is by licking them to death." She wraps her arms around the fluffball, places a kiss on the top of her head, and then leans down to place her on the ground. Picking up the ball Gypsy dropped, she throws it back toward the mudroom and we both watch her race after it, her claws clattering on the hardwood floor.

"Is pizza still your favorite? The local place is pretty fast, we can probably be eating in under an hour."

My ego gives a fist bump, realizing she remembers my favorite food. Which is ridiculous. I practically lived here growing up. Just because she remembers I love pizza doesn't mean anything.

"Yeah, pizza's great."

I watch her tap away on her phone, placing the order. Her other hand plays with a strand of her long hair and her normally wide eyes are narrowed as she stares at the screen. Her creamy skin has a perpetual rosiness along her cheekbones and she still has a smattering of freckles across her nose, just like she did when she was a kid.

I think back to the last time I saw her. It was her twenty-first birthday and I remember the exact moment I spotted her. She was moving through the room confidently, her face lit up with a huge smile, and it was like a punch to the face. The fresh-faced kid I remembered from five years earlier was gone and had been replaced by a woman I wanted in my bed.

Or in my car. Really, wherever she would have me.

Her small nose scrunches up. "Pineapple on pizza is so gross, Nick."

Well, would you look at that. She even remembers my exact order.

"Pineapple and sausage pizza is a gift from the gods. You should try it."

She presses a final button and drops her phone onto the counter. "I will *never* eat pineapple on pizza and, honestly, I don't entirely trust anyone who does."

I clutch my chest, wounded. "That hurts, Holly, that really hurts." Standing up, I stretch my arms above my head, my shoulders feeling tight from a long day at work.

A small sigh catches my attention and I look down to see Holly staring at my sweatpants. She runs her tongue lightly along her bottom lip and I feel my cock twitch in appreciation.

I clear my throat and try to hide a smirk. Everything in me wants to make a smart-ass comment. Flirt with her a little. But Brandon's warning from three years ago rings loudly in my head, *"keep your fucking hands off my sister, asshole. You're not even worthy of* looking *at her right now."*

I'm not going to lie, the chemistry between us is unexpected. I'm well aware of the attraction I felt to her, all those years ago, but I never expected to see the same interest reflected back at me. My gut clenches and I force myself to remember how Brandon stood by me when so many others disappeared. Starting something with his sister would be a dick move.

Instead, I ignore the heated moment and move to the refrigerator to grab a bottle of water.

Her stool screeches across the floor as she stands and I watch her from the corner of my eye awkwardly rub her chest.

"I'm going to go have a shower. Can you give me a shout when the pizza arrives?"

Without waiting for my answer, she turns and hotfoots it out of the room, leaving me with only an image of her naked and sudsy, and a bad feeling about how the next few days might play out.

I am halfway through my second slice when Holly bounds down the stairs in a pair of ass-hugging yoga pants and a sloppy orange sweater that's falling off one of her shoulders. The scent of peppermint infuses the air around her. I shift in my seat, putting my foot on the coffee table so my leg is slightly raised and hiding my semi.

Her hand runs along the tinsel tied to the banister as she skips down and I notice her roll her eyes.

"What was that?"

"What was what?" She heads straight for the pizza

boxes beside my foot and makes a gagging noise when the first box she opens has my pizza in it.

"You rolled your eyes at the tinsel. I'm not sure what an inanimate object could have done to deserve that kind of treatment."

"It's a Christmas decoration. It deserves that treatment just for existing." She takes a seat on the other end of the couch, and sits cross-legged, balancing a paper plate with two of her own slices on her lap.

Her comment rattles a memory loose and I suddenly have an image of fourteen-year-old Holly casually strolling into her family Christmas party wearing a *Santa is Satan* T-shirt. Her horrified grandparents promptly ushered her out of the party, much to her delight.

"Oh god, Santa is Satan." I almost choke on a laugh. "I had forgotten all about that."

A small smile plays on her lips, but she folds them between her teeth in an effort to hide it. "That was one of my better efforts. Nana and Papa were horrified." She gives up on hiding her smile and giggles. "But Mom and Dad respected my dedication and let me spend the rest of the night in my room." She grimaces at me. "The grandparents were *not* impressed with that."

We both go back to our food and, maybe it's just me, but there's an awkwardness between us that I hate.

It's funny, Holly and I have known each other most of our lives, but I can't remember a single time we have spent time alone like this.

Brandon and I became inseparable the day the

Curtises moved in next door to my family when we were eight. Since my parents worked so much we spent most of our time at his house. His mom was like a second mother to me, and even though his dad worked a lot, he was still around more than mine.

My memories of Holly aren't so clear though. I remember being curious about her when they first moved in. Being an only child, I wasn't sure how to behave around a little sister, which is how I assumed I should treat her. I always followed Brandon's lead, teasing her and playing jokes. But the older she got, the less she was around. In fact, the last few years before I left for college, it felt like she was leaving every room I entered.

I remember the dread I felt at the time, worried I had upset her. Selfishly concerned that it would mean my presence in their home would become unwelcome, and I'd have to go back to spending my nights in my own house. Where the laughter and warmth of the Curtises' would be replaced with silence and emptiness.

Brandon waved off my concerns and assured me it was nothing I had done. I had no reason not to trust him, so I did.

Her awkwardness now though, has all those doubts resurfacing, although this time for very different reasons.

I snag another couple of pieces of pizza and swing my legs up onto the sofa, nudging Holly's knee with my toes.

"What's the deal with hating Christmas? I feel like I

need to bah humbug you and pelt you with candy canes."

She immediately perks up. "Do you have any candy canes?"

"No." I laugh.

Her blue eyes narrow with a glare. "You really shouldn't get people's hopes up like that, you know."

"So, you're not against all Christmas traditions then? Good to know." I take a bite of pizza and watch her try to stutter a reply before taking pity on her. "I get it, if my birthday was Christmas Day, I'd hate it too."

She chews slowly and eyes me suspiciously. Whatever she sees on my face must soothe her, because she shrugs and looks away.

"It's childish and petty, I'm fully aware of that."

"Nah, everyone wants to feel special on their birthday." Honestly? I have no idea if that is true. I couldn't give a fuck about my birthday, but I'm not liking the look of unease on her face and I'll say anything to get rid of it.

"It's just" —she tosses her empty paper plate on the coffee table and turns to face me fully— "your birthday and Christmas are supposed to be the most magical days of the year when you're a kid." She pauses, chewing on her lip and staring off, just above my head. "But when your birthday is *on* Christmas, you kind of lose the magic of both days. Your birthday isn't special because everyone is too wrapped up in the holidays to really care about it, and then your resentment of Christmas steals the joy of *that* day. It's like you lose the magic of your childhood way too soon and it's just sad."

She exhales out a deep breath and groans. "God, that sounds so dramatic, ignore me." Shaking her head, she swipes the television remote off the table and turns the TV on.

I sit, staring at her, completely enthralled and a little heartbroken for Holly, the little girl who never experienced the same joy I did in my childhood.

My parents worked their asses off to give me the life they felt I deserved, so they were gone a lot. Too much, and I spent a lot of years angry at them for that. But my birthday and Christmas were the two days a year I could always count on them being there, from sunup to sundown. They were my favorite days of the year, and I hate that she never experienced the pure happiness those days are supposed to give children.

Holly leans forward, her eyes glued to the TV as she flicks through the channels, completely oblivious to the plan that is currently forming in my mind.

A plan that does not bode well for my promise to stay away from my best friend's sister.

"Holly," I start, grabbing her attention. "I have a proposal for you."

3

HOLLY

"Freaking sweatpants!" I shriek at Billie. "It's the sweatpant's fault. I was rendered useless by his dick print. It's the only explanation for why I agreed to this ridiculousness."

I snuggle into the cushions that Billie and I insist on keeping piled high on our couch, and tighten my hold on the mug of peppermint hot chocolate that is warming my fingers.

"I don't know," Billie muses from the kitchen where she's cleaning up. "From everything you've told me about *Nick*." She says his name in a swoony manner that I find highly offensive. "You would agree to anything he offered."

"That is not helpful." I sink lower into the sofa, pulling my knees up to my chest. My eyes follow her as she moves around the room and I have to stifle a sigh. She's been like this ever since she moved in almost a year ago. I wish she trusted that I asked her to be my roommate because I love her company. Not because I need a quasi housekeeper.

"And you just took off this morning without talking to him about his plan?"

"Will you stop, please." I wave my hand around in the general direction of the kitchen and pat the seat next to me. "Come and sit, so you can properly humor me."

I can practically feel her eye roll from the other side of the room, but she throws the cloth she was scrubbing the counters with into the sink and slowly makes her way over.

"Fine," she huffs, plopping down. "So, you were about to tell me how you ran away like a little bitch?"

The pillow behind my back comes in handy when I throw it at her.

"I didn't *run away*," I snap. "He was out when it was time for me to come here. It was just a happy coincidence."

"Holly." She levels me with a stare that has me wriggling in my seat. "I wasn't even awake when you got here, and Troy isn't dropping Tahlia off for another—" She glances at her watch. "Half an hour. You've been here for at least three hours longer than necessary. *At least.*"

God, she's such a smart-ass, why am I friends with her again?

"I needed to come over and make sure the apartment was clean and kid ready." I smile smugly and throw in a mental *so there*, because I'm a petty Betty.

"You have been sitting on your ass, drinking that

revolting peppermint chocolate concoction and reading trashy magazines since you got here."

"How do you know? You were fast asleep when I got here, lazybones," I challenge.

Okay, the lazy comment might have been a step too far. Billie's porcelain skin flushes a deep, angry red that makes her freckles stand out even more. When her nostrils start to flare, I know I'm in trouble.

"Lazy? I was sleeping because I worked until two in the morning at the pizzeria, *after* working a full day at *Avondale*, I might add, and today is the first day off I've had in five weeks." She kicks her foot out at me, catching me on my shin, inflicting the pain I deserve. "Lazy, my ass, you shithead."

Giving my shin a rub, I throw her a wide-eyed look, feeling awful. "I'm sorry, I didn't mean it. I'm all off-kilter because of Nick," I groan. "Maybe I should just come back home while he's staying there?"

Billie grabs up a magazine off the coffee table and starts thumbing through it. "I don't know, it's like he said, what's the point? If he's only going to be there a couple of days, it seems like it would be more trouble than it's worth." She glances up at me. "Is his plan really so terrible?"

"He wants to teach me to love Christmas, Billie. That—that's," I stutter incredulously, trying to think of a way to verbalize the ludicrousness of his proposition. "Impossible! It's *impossible*. I've tried to enjoy Christmas and it never works. But he thinks he's going to waltz into my life, with his dreamy green eyes and his chiseled jaw... his muscly arms with that sleeve of tattoos... God, what is it about tattoos that is such a turn on?"

"I feel like you're going off on a bit of a tangent there, Hols." Billie's eyes stay glued to the pages in her lap. "And, also, you might need to cut back on the romance novels."

"What? Oh." I give my head a small shake to clear it before leaning down to put my empty mug on the table. "Okay, here's the thing."

"Tell me the thing. God, *please*, tell me the thing." My roommate licks her thumb and turns the page while side-eyeing me.

"I don't appreciate your sarcasm, Billie, but frankly, I'm too desperate to care." She snorts out a laugh which, again, I choose to ignore. "I've had a crush on Nick since I was eight years old and I watched him tackle my brother in a game of backyard football."

"But you hate football," Billie interrupts, finally turning her attention from the magazine to me.

"I know!" I shriek. "It's the Nick effect! From that moment on, everything he did turned me into a stuttering idiot. I couldn't form complete sentences around him, which was so humiliating. That was the start of almost a decade where I simultaneously avoided him and sought him out. It was exhausting." Even just the memory of those years has my shoulders slumping.

"Hmmm, it sounds like it." I look up to see I've lost her again, and she's engrossed in an article about the best blow job positions.

"Please, when do you have time to be giving blow jobs?" I snark.

"You can never be too prepared," she murmurs, completely ignoring my attempt at sarcasm.

"Forget it," I mumble and fold my arms across my chest. I bite my bottom lip when I realize it's sticking out and I'm pouting like a two-year-old.

Billie holds a finger up at me and her eyes skim the rest of the article while I try to remember I am a grown-up and I really should start acting like it.

"Okay." Billie closes the magazine and tosses it back on the table, turning to face me. "You now have my undivided attention. Go."

"It's just, it was only ever a crush, you know? He was off-limits. Kind of quiet and broody. He got in fights and seemed angry a lot of the time." A million memories of him over the years flash through my mind, and I wonder briefly how many he has of me. "It's such a cliche, but he was the bad boy and it really did something for me."

Billie purses her lips, quirking an eyebrow at me. "That doesn't sound like the Holly I know."

"I know. Nick O'Connor was the exception to my every rule." I smile ruefully, shaking my head. "It doesn't matter though, he never knew I existed." I blink away an unwelcome image of Nick looking right through me. It was the only way he ever looked at me growing up. I was always just Brandon's kid sister. "Anyway, he was always just a fantasy. But last night he was different."

"How so?"

"He was funny and just, I don't know, he seemed sort of *lighter*." I shrug. "He was... real." I chew my bottom lip, not liking this feeling of vulnerability. "When a fantasy doesn't know you exist, it doesn't really hurt because your feelings aren't based in reality, does that make sense?"

She nods, her eyes narrowed and I try to ignore the look of concern that is starting to creep onto her face.

"When you have feelings for a real person, and they don't see you, it kind of sucks."

Billie holds my gaze wearing an expression I can't quite decipher.

"Maybe you should—"

She is cut off by a loud bang on the front door, followed by a shrill voice screeching, "Auntie Holly! We're gonna go see Santa!"

My mouth drops and I rush to the door, completely prepared to break a five-year-old's heart. Because, babysitting? Yes.

Santa? No. Just, no.

"His beard is so shiny." Tahlia's eyes look like they are about to pop out of her head and her tiny body is vibrating with excitement.

Mine is vibrating more with annoyance.

"I'm sorry, Hols. She was mad that we're going out without her and the only way we could get her to leave the house was to promise you would take her to see Santa." Troy's explanation still sounds hollow all these hours later.

I mean, I think this would have been a perfect

opportunity to teach her that you can't always get your own way, but what do I know? According to Troy, I'm childless, so my opinion has no merit.

"It is, isn't it? I bet Mrs. Claus insists he uses a beard conditioner on it." I nod authoritatively.

Tahlia scrunches up her perky little nose at me. "I think it's probably just magic, Auntie Holly." She looks away and I don't know if I'm being oversensitive, but I get the distinct impression that I just embarrassed a five-year-old.

I tighten my hold on Tahlia's hand and look around the Santa village for what feels like the hundredth time in the last hour. It's a cacophony of children yelling, irritating Christmas carols, and complaints mumbled under the breath of aggravated parents.

Can you imagine a happier place on earth?

Insert eye roll here, please.

"So, what are you going to ask Santa for, Tahls?"

"A microscope and a fairy light garden." She starts swinging our joined hands and when the child ahead of us takes his turn on Santa's lap and we step up to the front of the line, she actually squees. I didn't realize that was even a real sound until this moment.

"I wonder if Santa will remember you from last year?" I do my best to infuse my voice with excitement.

Tahlia just looks at me, tilting her head to the side, and I feel as though I'm being judged. Harshly.

"You know he's not the *real* Santa, right, Holly?"

What the hell happened to *Auntie* Holly? Is this what it feels like to be dumped by an honorary niece?

"Oh, yeah, of course, I mean, I just wasn't sure if you knew that," I fumble.

"I'm *five*, I'm not a baby." She does this weird kind of disappointed headshake at me, and suddenly I remember the last time I was at a Santa village.

I was eleven and talking to my best friend about my upcoming birthday. The girl ahead of us, Marcy, who was truly awful by the way, turned around and snapped at me, "Will you shut up about your stupid birthday? It's Christmas, no one cares!"

I wanted the ground to open up and swallow me then, and I want it to open up and swallow me now. Albeit for different reasons.

"Right, right, right. So… why are you so excited if you know he's not the real thing?"

"I'm doing an 'xperment."

"'Xperment?" I'm so confused right now.

"Yep, my daddies told me these are Santa's helpers, so I'm asking each one I see for something different so I can see who is the best helper."

"Oh, an experiment!"

"That's what I said." She takes a step away from me and I fear that I am dangerously close to losing hand holding privileges.

"Wait, how many Santas have you seen?"

"One, two, three, four." She holds up four fingers.

"Four?!" *I am going to kill Troy.*

"Next, please." A grim-faced teenage girl dressed up as an elf, approaches and motions for us to take our turn with Santa.

Santa number five.

"Hey Santa!" All trace of her annoyance with me vanishes as Tahlia rushes up the steps and launches herself on his lap.

"Ho! Ho! Ho! Merry Christmas! Have you been a good girl this year?"

"I've been super good, Santa." She starts scrambling around in the tiny purse she insisted on bringing and pulls out a small piece of paper. "My daddies had to have a date today, so Holly brought me, but Dad wrote me a letter to give to you, so you know how good I've been."

"That's, well, that's very helpful." Confused eyes meet mine and all I can do is shrug. I'm taking no part in this farce.

"Uh huh. I'm very helpful, aren't I, Auntie Holly?"

Oh, sure, *now* I'm Auntie Holly.

"You sure are. Tahlia, how about you tell Santa what you want, quick sticks. There's still a lot of kids waiting to see him."

Tossing me a look of what could only be described as exasperation, she quickly goes through her list and when Santa assures her that he'll do the best he can, I prepare to take her hand and hightail it out of this Christmas nightmare.

"It's your turn, Auntie Holly." Tahlia hops off his lap and then motions for me to take her place.

"Oh god, no." The words slip out before I can stop them. "I mean, no thank you, Tahls, only kids sit on Santa's lap. C'mon, let's go and let the next person have their turn."

"No, you have to have your turn, Holly." Her voice takes on a whiny quality that I could really do without.

"It's okay, it's more common than you think." Santa pats his lap in what I'm sure he considers an inviting manner. Me? I just find it creepy.

"No, thanks." My voice takes on a shrill tone that makes me cringe.

"Holly, sit. Down!" Tahlia hisses, as though I'm the one embarrassing her.

Could this moment be any more horrific?

I probably shouldn't have tempted fate with that thought. Because when I look helplessly around the perimeter of the village to all the people standing behind the tiny picket fence, my eyes clash with a pair of beautiful jade ones that are watching me curiously while a smirk plays across his lips.

What the hell is Nick doing at Santa's village?

4

NICK

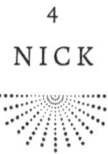

*J*t's a standoff and I feel like I am being supremely outwitted.

"It's mine." Tahlia glares at me. "I'm a little kid *and* I'm the guest, so you have to let me have the last marshmallow."

"I'm also a guest here and I'm your elder, so I would argue that means *I* get to have the last marshmallow."

She scowls at me across the dining table where Holly set us up before rushing off to make a call.

"You're lucky though, because I am also a gentleman, so you can have the last one." I push the almost empty bag across to her and enjoy the grin that lights up her face.

"Thank you, Nick," she replies, suddenly demure as she stuffs the marshmallow in her already overflowing cup of hot chocolate.

While Tahlia is distracted, I steal a look across at Holly, who is leaning against the kitchen island. Biting her nails and with a furrowed brow, she looks worried, and an instinct to fix whatever the problem is propels me off my seat and headed in her direction.

"Is he going to be okay?" She glances up at me as I take a spot next to her. "Mmmhmm..." She nods, worrying her bottom lip with her teeth. "Of course she can stay, keep me updated and give Troy my love." Her lips turn up in a smirk and I am suddenly aware of how close I'm standing. How easy it would be to run my thumb along that lush bottom lip that I fantasize about a little too often. "You can also warn him that I plan on teasing him mercilessly when I see him."

A low rumble on the other end of the line has her giggling and I feel my cock come to life at the sound. I really should move away, but she smells so good. Ironically, like Christmas. Peppermint and chocolate.

Edible.

Coming to my senses, I take a step back and move around to the other side of the counter to hide my semi. I wonder if it would look suspicious if I carry a book in front of my crotch whenever I'm around her.

Hell, it worked in eighth grade around Shauna Garrett.

"So, apparently Troy was showing off his moves on the ice-skating rink and has hurt his ankle."

Holly's voice jolts me from my thoughts and I look up to find her trying to smother a laugh. "He's fine, but they're at the hospital waiting to get it looked at. I hope it's okay with you, I said Tahlia could sleep here tonight. Give them one less thing to worry about." She shrugs apologetically. "I can take her back to the apartment so she's not in your hair. I didn't actually intend to bring her here today, I promise."

That much was obvious when she tried to bolt after I stumbled across her at the mall.

In a Santa village.

Surrounded by fake snow, gingerbread houses, and life-sized candy canes.

I'm pretty sure it was my heaven and her hell.

Luckily, it only took one mention of Gypsy to have Tahlia insisting on coming back to the house to visit her. Otherwise I'm sure Holly would have disappeared faster than I could say Ho! Ho! Ho!

I glance across to Tahlia who is studiously slurping up her drink, chocolate covering her face, hands sticky with marshmallow goo and a hopeful dog sitting at her feet.

"She's no bother, I don't mind if she stays." I chance a quick look at my watch and see it's just after two. "I need to head into my workshop for a few hours anyway."

"You have a workshop? Color me impressed." Her eyes sparkle mischievously.

Sparkle mischievously? Who the hell am *I?*

"Brandon mentioned you had started your own business, how's it going?"

I wonder briefly if she's been asking about me.

"It's been good. It was tough at first, the custom furniture business is built on reputation, so starting from scratch, it took a while to get my name out there. But business has been steadily increasing, so I've got no complaints."

"That's great, Nick, I'm happy for you. I know things were tough when—"

"Yeah, I'm good now though." I reach up and knead the knot in my neck that suddenly feels uncomfortably tight.

"Right." She averts her eyes and the air in the room shifts, a tension that wasn't there a moment ago now hanging heavy.

"Well, I'm glad." She offers me a small smile. "It's probably best that you're heading out. I thought Tahlia and I could make some sugar cookies, so this place is going to be a complete mess in about fifteen minutes."

"Cookies?" I practically groan. Cookies are my weakness.

"Who's having cookies?" Tahlia shrieks and Gypsy barks in support.

Holly grimaces. "Maybe more sugar isn't such a good idea..."

Oh, hell no. I can tolerate wanting a woman I can't have, I am a grown man after all. But cookies are an entirely different matter.

If she is throwing around the suggestion of cookies, then I'm sorry, but I'm going to need those cookies.

"Who's having cookies?" I throw Tahlia's question back at her as I move through the kitchen. Reaching the dining table, I grab Tahlia up, offering her my hand for a hi-five. "We are, kid. We are."

This has definitely not been one of my better ideas.

The last forty-five minutes have tested my resolve, my willpower, and my commitment to an eighteen-year friendship.

Despite the temperature outside, the kitchen heated up as soon as the oven was on and Holly took this as a cue to strip down to leggings and a tank top. Her curvy ass and ample tits were on display, and it took every ounce of my self-control to keep my hands to myself.

Every move she made reminded me how much I want her.

Every move she made reminded me how much of an asshole I am.

It didn't help that she kept touching me. A brush of her fingers here, the graze of her arm there.

I feel drunk on her. I both loathe and love it at the same time.

"Nick!" Tahlia's voice snaps me back to reality. "I need the sprinkles."

I pass her the container as I survey the damage that's been done to the kitchen. Ingredients cover the island and flour seems to coat everything, including the three of us, while dishcloths cover the ground to sop up spills.

Despite the chaos, the room is filled with the sweet scent of cookies and my mouth practically waters as I watch Holly bend over and pull the cookie sheet out of the oven.

Don't ask me if it's the cookies or Holly that has me wiping my chin, I don't think I could tell you.

"Tahlia, I want you to run to the bathroom and clean up while the cookies cool down," Holly instructs.

Tahlia opens her mouth to argue, but she quickly shuts it when she sees the look Holly throws her.

"Fine."

The sound of her feet sliding across the floor is followed by the clatter of claws as Gypsy follows her.

"Oh my god." Holly slumps against the counter and buries her face in her hands. "This was such a shitty idea."

I can't stop my laugh when she glances up and I see the expression on her face.

"Look at this place!" She throws her arms up in defeat before pointing an accusing finger at me. "Why did you let me do this?"

"This was all you, Curtis, I take no responsibility for any of it."

She sighs deeply and nods, pulling a face. "I am a stupid, stupid woman."

"C'mon." I reach out and grab her hand.

Mistake. *Big mistake.*

Electricity hums under my skin the second I touch her and instead of simply moving toward the mess, she steps into me, bringing herself flush up against my chest.

Her hair smells like peppermint and when she looks up at me, her cheeks are flushed. Wide-eyed, she raises a hand and places it over my heart, which is racing almost painfully.

All I can think about is kissing her. I fixate on her mouth, the shape of it, my eyes tracing the curve of her full bottom lip, wondering what it would taste like.

I lower my head toward her, so close—*so close*—to satisfying my curiosity.

Her breath hitches and that one small sound is enough to bring me back to my senses.

I jerk back, swallowing roughly against the look of disappointment that immediately clouds her features.

I clear my throat, regret already overwhelming me. "Uh, I really need to get to the workshop." I start to back away. "Leave the mess, I'll clean it up when I get back."

Without waiting for a response, I turn and make my way out of the house.

❦

"Okay, I'm here, this better be good, I was just heading home to a beer with my name on it."

Cohen, my accountant and one of my best friends, pushes through the double doors to my workshop and glowers at me.

"I just put some bottles in there." I gesture to the freestanding refrigerator I have shoved in the corner of the room.

He grabs a drink and comes to sit beside me on one of the old deck chairs I keep for emergencies like this.

Silently, Cohen opens his bottle and takes a slug, keeping his eyes glued to me. "What's going on, man? You haven't called a meeting of the brain trust in a couple of years."

"You're my brain trust?" I lift a questioning eyebrow.

"Clearly. I don't see Brandon anywhere." Cohen and Brandon's competitiveness is legendary, they've been battling it out for alpha status since we were teenagers and I can tell he's loving the idea of coming out on top today.

"Firstly, Brandon's out of town so he couldn't be here, even if I wanted him to." I take a pull of my beer and then scrub a hand across my mouth. "Secondly, I can't talk to him about this, so you're the brain trust by default. Go you." I try to grin at him to soften the blow, but it's a struggle.

"Ah, then the topic of today must be young Holly Curtis. Gotta say, it's been a while since I had to listen to you pine over her. I kind of thought you were over it."

"She's not young," I grunt. "She's only a couple of years younger than us, her age isn't the problem. And, there's nothing to get over."

"Then why am I here? On a Saturday afternoon when I could be at home watching a game, why am I in your smelly workshop surrounded by varnish, wood shavings, and power tools?" He smooths a hand over his suit, that no doubt is the most expensive thing in this room.

"I almost kissed her."

That catches him off guard and he spits out a mouthful of beer.

"How the fuck did that happen? Where did you even see her?" He wipes his chin.

"There's some plumbing problems with my building, and I'm staying at Brandon's for a few days." I wait a beat before dropping the bombshell. "With Holly."

I watch him closely for his reaction, but aside from a slight flaring of his nostrils, he gives me nothing.

We stare at each other silently and I can't get a read on him.

Finally, I can't take it anymore. "Nothing?" I bite out. "I thought you'd have a hell of a lot to say about that."

Cohen stares a few moments longer and then exhales a deep sigh.

"I don't really understand how this happened."

"What's to understand? My super called on Friday and told me about a plumbing emergency. I was given an hour to run home and grab some things, so then I called Brandon to see if I could stay with him for a few days. I forgot that he and Amy were visiting her parents, but he said I was welcome to stay." I shake my head, replaying the conversation in my head. "Just before I hung up, he told me Holly was house-sitting for them, but he was sure she wouldn't mind. It would have looked strange if I suddenly didn't need a place as soon as he told me she was there." My voice sounds defensive even to my own ears.

He nods slowly, deep in thought. Needing to keep my hands occupied, I grab a piece of wood and a knife off my work table and start whittling away.

"I think you could have easily said you would stay at my place or even a hotel without it looking suspicious." Cohen meets my eye and holds it determinedly. "You chose to stay there with her because you wanted to. Man up and admit it."

My hands stop moving and I fight back against my gut reaction to deny his accusation. But he's right. When Brandon told me Holly was house-sitting, I suddenly couldn't wait to get there.

"I'll take your silence as a concession." Cohen's voice is entirely too smug. "You have feelings for her, Nick. If you can't even make it twenty-four hours without making a move on her, then that's pretty damn obvious."

"I don't have *feelings* for her, I'm attracted to her. There's a big difference."

"That's all it is? Really? Because for the last three years, she's been the bar you've set for yourself. You pulled yourself up out of the gutter after you saw her that night. You got your life back on track because you wanted to be worthy of a woman like her." He narrows his eyes. "Don't you think it's about time you admit to yourself that it's *her* you want to be worthy of?"

That night flashes through my mind, and it is almost painful to remember how it changed my life and set me on a new course.

How I've denied myself what I really wanted while doing everything in my power to be deserving of it.

Cohen's right, I do want her. All of her.

The only question now, is what the fuck am I going to do about it?

5

NICK

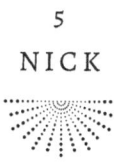

hree years ago...

The Uber pulls up in front of a large house and the familiarity strikes me deep in my gut. It's lit up like nothing I have ever seen before, and noise from inside filters through into the car. My head throbs, a sign I'm more sober than I like to be these days and it's only the thought of beer, or better yet, whiskey, that forces me to thank the driver and get my ass out of the car.

It sure as hell isn't the idea of seeing Brandon, who most likely will want to kill me for showing up to Holly's twenty-first half drunk.

Having second thoughts, I turn back to the car just in time to see it disappear down the street.

Probably for the best. He would do more damage if I didn't show up at all.

The air is biting and by the time I reach—stumble

to—the front door, my bones feel frozen and the chill that has settled in my chest is unnerving.

The door handle turns easily, and I walk into a crowd of people, some standing around, some wandering aimlessly through the rooms I practically grew up in.

Memories start to come at me and my mouth is Sahara-desert dry. Searching for something that will relieve the ache, I spot a makeshift bar setup in what is normally the formal dining room. I make a beeline for it and help myself to a beer.

"You made it." My best friend's voice rises above the din of the room and I take a quick draw on my drink before turning to face the music.

"You're late—" His eyes move across my face, and I absently raise a hand and scrub it across my jaw. The stubble I didn't bother to shave when I woke up three hours ago is coarse against my hand. "Jesus, are you drunk?"

"No." Not yet, anyway.

"Well, you're not fucking sober."

He's got me there.

"You told me to come, so here I am, get off my ass, Brandon." I shake my head. "I don't know why I bothered. She's not my sister. This isn't my family." My voice breaks painfully on the word family, and I look away, sucking down more beer to stop the burn behind my eyes.

"You're here because we are family, Nick. I know it's been hard—"

"You don't know shit," I mutter. Refusing to look

him in the eye, I let my attention stray to the crowd. When my eyes land on a beautiful brunette walking through the cluster of people, I can't stop my smirk.

Maybe tonight won't be a complete waste after all.

"Are you fucking kidding me?" Brandon's harsh voice drags me back to him and I see his eyes glued to where I was just looking. "My sister? You turn up to her birthday party hungover, if not drunk, and then look at her like she's a piece of ass you're gonna use for a night before tossing away?"

I glower at his accusation. Holly? There's no way that girl with the tits and ass is the same kid I last saw five years ago. I swing my head back around until I spot her again, determined to find Holly somewhere nearby. Squinting, I spot my girl, and a slow wave of awareness forms into a cold, hard ball of dread in the pit of my stomach. Closing my eyes, I take a second to clear my head before opening them. It's like a slap to the face when I realize that underneath the curves and the makeup, I was just fantasizing about fucking my best friend's kid sister.

This is quite possibly the lowest I've sunk yet.

A rough hand on my shoulder yanks me back around to face Brandon.

"I know you're having a tough time right now, but keep your fucking hands off my sister, asshole. You're not even worthy of looking at her right now."

He pushes past me harshly before disappearing into the crowd.

I should follow him and apologize. I should put this

drink down and sober up for the first time in months. There are a lot of things I should do.

Instead I down the last of my beer and crack open another one.

The chains of the swing set creak as I push myself back and forth. I'm probably about to break the damn thing but I don't have it in me to care.

It's dark back here in the corner of the yard, and I like the feeling of anonymity that blankets me. Like I'm invisible.

Nobody needs to see me, or what I've become, right now.

A twig breaking snaps me out of my stupor and I look up to see a vision walking toward me.

I might be drunker than I thought.

"Nick?" Her voice is soft, barely a whisper, and she holds a bulky jacket in her arms.

"Hey." My voice is raspy, so I clear my throat and try again. "What are you doing back here? You should be up there celebrating your birthday with all your friends."

"Pfft, my birthday is next week, not today," she huffs cutely and shoves the jacket at me. "I thought you might be cold."

For the first time, I notice that I'm in a T-shirt. Probably not the best thing to wear outside in the middle of the night in mid-December.

"Thanks," I mumble, slipping the jacket on, suddenly freezing.

She takes a seat on the swing next to me, but I can feel her gaze burning into the side of my face.

"Thank you for coming."

"Brandon didn't give me much choice." I chuckle, but immediately wish I could take it back when she dips her head in embarrassment.

"Of course he didn't." She wraps her arms around herself and for a moment it looks like she's trying to protect herself. From me?

"You don't have to stay." She gives me a small smile. "You've done your duty."

I am an asshole.

"I didn't mean it like that, Hols. Of course I want to be here."

She stares up at me and she's so fucking pretty I almost don't know what to do with myself. Her eyes are sapphire blue that seem darker out here under the stars, and I don't know why, but I have this urgent need to memorize everything about this moment. As though a fundamental part of me recognizes its importance, even if I can't quite understand what that is.

We sit on the swings, side by side, and when she begins to gently rock herself back and forth causing the chains to creak, I'm grateful for the distraction. The silence I welcomed only moments ago feels stifling with Holly beside me.

"I'm sorry about your dad."

It's a statement. Straightforward and not requiring

a response. Thank fuck, because I can't seem to work my tongue loose enough to give her one.

"I heard him talking to my dad about you once, you know?"

I glance over at her to find she is looking up at the stars, her expression unreadable.

"He loved you so much, but he was worried he was messing it all up. He wanted to give you everything he never had and the only way he knew how to do that was to work his backside off." She bites her bottom lip and her nose twitches as though she's holding back tears. "My dad told him you were a good kid and maybe you didn't always understand why he worked so much then, but one day you would and you would thank him for it." She leans her head against the chain and a small sigh escapes her plump lips. "Maybe if he knew how little time he had, he would have made different choices, but god, Nick, his heart was in the most beautiful place."

I choke down a swallow, and all I can get out is a strangled, "I know."

There is a pause, a moment when we're both lost in memories, before I can't do it anymore. I open my mouth to change the subject, but before I can, Holly cuts me to the quick.

"Then how about you pull your head out of your ass and get your fucking life together."

Well, punch me in the dick and call me Sally, who the fuck is this girl?

"Brandon told me you lost your job." She shakes her head and throws an anguished look my way. "About the drinking. You barely talk to your mom. He'd be so disappointed," she ends with a whisper. I don't have to ask who she's talking about.

Anger instinctively rushes through me. I want to tell her to fuck off, tell her that she doesn't know shit about the relationship I have—had—with my parents. But she does. Of course she does, she was there for most of it.

My eyes fall to my feet because looking at Holly feels too difficult right now.

"I was mad at my parents a lot growing up. I resented how often they were gone. I mean, logically, I knew they were doing it for the right reasons, but I was a kid." I clear my throat. "I just wanted them *there*. When they got divorced after I left for college I wasn't surprised. I *was* surprised when Dad moved to Washington and started turning up at my door every Sunday for dinner." Memory after memory hits me but instead of the painful bite of anger, I feel grateful for each and every one of them. "I didn't know he'd had a heart attack. I didn't know that's what instigated the changes he made. The new job, making more of an effort to spend time with me, all of it." The unforgiving burn behind my eyes causes me to scrub a hand over my face. "He should have told me."

"Would it have changed anything?"

"I would have been prepared," I snap. "He should have prepared me for this happening, I had no fucking clue."

"Maybe." Uncertainty clouds her words and I find myself seeking out her eyes. "Or maybe he didn't want you to worry. Maybe he wanted to just enjoy the relationship he was building with you." She stills, turning to face me. "Or maybe he didn't think things were as serious as they were. You'll never know."

I huff out a bitter laugh, because isn't that the point? I'll never have answers now.

"You and I both know there wasn't a malicious bone in your dad's body. Whatever his reasons were, you know—*you know*—they were honorable. So what are you going to do? Hate him forever because he didn't do things the way *you* think he should? Fuck your life up just to defy him? What the hell does that achieve?"

Her anger is palpable and I'm a little afraid right now.

"He made amends for his mistakes, Nick, and he turned his entire life upside down to do it. It's time for you to grow the fuck up and forgive him. Be the man he raised you to be, not the drunken asshole you've become."

Have you ever been called out so hard you don't know whether to cuss the person out and storm off or fall to your knees in gratitude at being seen?

Yeah, until this moment I hadn't either.

Choking down the lump in my throat, I finally put words to what I have been struggling with for all these months. "If I don't hold on to this anger, then I'll have to start moving on." I tighten my grip on the chains of the swing. "I'm not ready to let him go yet."

She reaches out and strokes her thumb over my cheek, claiming a tear I didn't even realize had fallen. "You don't have to let him go. But hold on to him with love, not hate. Be grateful for every moment you had with him, instead of angry for every moment you missed out on."

My eyes trace over every inch of her face, taking in the details I had never noticed before. From the dusting of freckles that cover her nose to the silvery scar that runs along her temple, I'm struck with the sudden need to memorize each and every one as though they are vital to my existence.

"When did you get so smart?"

She smiles softly. "I'm pretty damn special, Nick O'Connor, you just never bothered to notice."

I'm definitely noticing now.

Before I can articulate the thought, she bounces up off the swing and starts to walk away.

But not before throwing a challenge over her shoulder.

"Get your shit together, Nick, and maybe one day you'll deserve a girl like me."

6

HOLLY

*D*o you know how many times you can walk from the kitchen to the living room in this house, in two hours? Four hundred and twenty-three.

How do I know this? Because I have been pacing that very path, back and forth, since I put Tahlia to bed.

I can't stop my brain from replaying that moment with Nick in the kitchen, over and over and... well, you get the point.

He was going to kiss me. I *know* he was going to kiss me.

So, why didn't he?

I'm midway through lap four hundred and twenty-four when I hear a key in the front door and I run to the sofa in the living room like the hounds of hell are at my feet.

I have just gotten myself situated with a bowl of untouched popcorn on my lap when he appears. He gives me a lazy grin and I give him a quick once-over, doing my best to be subtle.

He's in the same dark jeans and black T-shirt he was wearing earlier, the T-shirt molded to his broad chest and thick biceps. The artwork tattooed on his left arm catches my attention, and I wonder if I'll ever get the chance to learn the story of each piece.

He doesn't look any worse for the wear, slightly more rumpled than before, but nothing that tells me he was out doing something he would regret.

"What are you watching?" His voice is deeper than usual. Rough, the way it always used to sound first thing in the morning. God, I lived for the moments I would hear that voice growing up.

"Uh." I throw a quick glance at the television screen and see an episode of *Friends* playing. *The One Where Nana Dies Twice.* Classic. "Friends." I wave a piece of popcorn at the TV.

"Huh, I've never seen it." He stalks across the room, flops onto the other end of the sofa and immediately starts pulling his Chucks off.

I'm fixated on the flex of his forearms, so it takes a moment for his comment to hit home.

"Wait, you've *never* seen *Friends*? Like, ever?" I don't even try to hide the disgust in my voice.

He reaches over and scoops a handful of popcorn out from the bowl between my legs, causing me to have a momentary lapse of concentration when I imagine his hand right there, doing decidedly dirtier things.

"You're sounding kind of judgy there, Hols."

"Oh, I am judging you. Harshly."

"Ouch." He clutches his chest. "I mean, I was born

the year it started and was still firmly obsessed with cartoons when it ended, so it's not that shocking."

"It's a classic, Nicholas," I state primly, shocked at what I am discovering and suddenly second-guessing this sixteen-year crush. "I mean, you have Nick at Nite, right? I don't know anyone who hasn't seen at least one episode of *Friends*. You know..." I pop a piece of buttery popcorn in my mouth and tap my chin thoughtfully. "There's probably some academic out there somewhere who would like to study your brain to find out what's lacking."

He looks at the screen and watches as Ross falls into an empty grave, his eyebrows raising. "Okay, Obi-Wan, tell me what's so great about it."

"I mean, well, it's just," I stammer, trying to put its excellence into words. "It's just so funny. It's almost thirty years old, and it's just as funny now as it was then. How many shows can say that? Most are dated only a few years after they screen. The jokes, the fashion, but *Friends* still feels relatable, even after all this time. God, I don't want to think about all the hours Billie and I have spent watching it when we should have been adulting."

Nick makes a nondescript sound, shaking his head slightly. "If you say so."

"Oh my god." I snatch up the remote and click back to the menu, cueing up the pilot episode. "I won't be able to live with myself if I don't educate you while I have the chance." Pressing play, I turn to him with a grin. "Welcome to Friends 101, Nick O'Connor. It sucks, you're gonna love it."

"Wha—"

"Just watch, that'll totally make sense in twenty minutes."

❧

"Okay, Ross and Rachel, they happen, right? Tell me they become a thing."

We've just finished *The One With Mrs. Bing*, and I think it's safe to say I have a convert on my hands.

"Oh yeah, it's a wild ride." I laugh.

"That Ross, man, he's kind of strange, but I think I love him."

"Yes!" I whisper-yell, conscious of Tahlia asleep upstairs. "Look, Chandler will always be my favorite, but Ross is a certain kind of crazy and I am so here for it."

Nick chuckles. "What's your favorite episode?"

I don't even have to think about my answer. "The one where Chandler proposes to Monica. It's just so romantic, these two characters who are normally so neurotic being all honest and heartfelt and *they're* crying and *I* cry every time I watch it." Embarrassingly, I feel myself start to tear up just thinking about it. "The room is so beautiful, with candles everywhere and it's just an unexpectedly perfect moment."

He's staring at me silently, and it takes me a second to realize that his attention is locked on my mouth. I have to resist the urge to lick my lips, not wanting to break the spell between us.

There's a shift in the room, the air thickens and

anticipation crawls up my spine, reminding me of the near kiss from earlier today.

My heart is racing, but before either one of us can act on any impulse, a small cry from upstairs breaks the tension.

"Tahlia?"

"Yeah, I put her down in my bed. I better go check on her."

"You want to keep watching? I'll make another bowl of popcorn."

"Sure." I hop up and leave the room before he sees the smile spread across my face.

Taking the stairs two at a time, I creep toward the guest room I've been staying in, not wanting to wake up Tahlia if she's still asleep.

I peek through the doorway. The room is dimly lit by the hallway light and I spot Tahlia snuggled up in the covers. She moves restlessly for a few moments before settling down, the sound of her soft snores filling the room. I spot Gypsy fast asleep at the foot of the bed, and they both look so cute while sleeping that I have to resist the urge to go over and smooch on them both.

Once I'm sure Tahlia isn't going to wake up, I decide to give myself a moment before I go back down to Nick. Heading to the bathroom, I play the last few hours out in my head.

Stepping inside the small tiled room, I'm immediately struck with the vision of a naked Nick, water dripping down his naked skin. His naked six-pack flexing as he dried his hair. Naked.

Did I mention he was naked?

I splash some cold water on my face, letting the coolness do its job and wake me up. I feel like the last few hours have lulled me into an alternate reality where Nick and I are actual friends, not strangers who are only connected by my brother. We've spent them talking about anything and everything, catching up on the last few years of our lives and reminiscing over memories I had long forgotten. We even touched on his dad and I'm so happy to see how much better he's doing. Such a huge difference from the last time I saw him.

Our conversation has made me realize that I spent so many years avoiding him, so desperately worried that I was going to humiliate myself in front of him, that I missed out on actually getting to know him. All those years I wasted crushing on a pretty face, when I could have been discovering what a good person he is.

Because hearing about it from Brandon is one thing, but seeing it for myself is something else entirely. The way he lavishes attention on Gypsy when he thinks I'm not looking, or the way he was so patient with Tahlia today. Those small acts show me who he really is.

He's the type of man I want.

He *is* the man I want.

NICK

· · ·

The seconds on the microwave countdown to zero and I try to clear my mind of everything but the sound of the popcorn popping and the buttery smell overpowering the kitchen.

It seemed so easy back in my workshop with Cohen encouraging me. Make a move and see if Holly feels the same way. If she does, go from there. If she doesn't, beg her not to confess my betrayal to Brandon.

Fuck. Is it a betrayal? Here in Brandon's home, it doesn't seem so straightforward anymore, and the realization that I might be risking my friendship is finally sinking in.

I grab the bowl from the sink and refill it with popcorn, shoving a handful in my mouth as I head back into the living room.

Last night and tonight have only confirmed what I suspected at Holly's birthday party. She's the trifecta: smart, funny, and beautiful and when I'm around her, it feels *right*.

As I settle back onto the sofa to wait for Holly to come back down, I make peace with what I'm about to do. Because the one thing I have no doubt about?

Holly is worth risking it all for.

7

HOLLY

"*A*re you ready?"

"Oh, crap!" I jump as I spill my hot choco-late, barely missing the front of my sweater, and throw a filthy look over my shoulder. I'm met with a set of smiling eyes that are far too perky looking for this early in the morning.

"Not much of a morning person, are you?" Nick comes up behind me and fills a thermos with coffee.

"I'll have you know that I normally love mornings. But I also normally get more than three hours sleep, so there is that."

"Whose fault is that?" He twists the top of the thermos tight and turns to look at me.

"Aren't you going to add milk and sugar to that?" I scrunch up my nose, because, ew. He just laughs at me, so I go on, ignoring him. "If I remember correctly, it was *you* who kept insisting just one more episode for approximately, hmm…" I tilt my head to the side as if thinking hard. "Twenty episodes. *And*, it was the five-year-old who has more energy than a red bull addict, who woke me up at five a.m." I close my eyes and groan, reliving the moment I was woken by a child and a dog, jumping on my bed, yelling and barking. I'll let you decide who was doing what.

"Are you going to tell me where we're going yet?"

"No." He winks at me, smirking. "But I will say that today is day one of *'Get Holly in the Christmas spirit'*."

I groan again, longer and louder this time. Who wants to waste their Sunday on *Christmas*. Bleurgh.

"We've got a bit of a drive, so we should probably get going, if you're ready."

"Fine," I grumble. Bending down to where Gypsy has been camped out by my feet, hoping to catch any breakfast crumbs, I give her a quick kiss on the head and make my way to the front door. "All right, let's get this over with so I can salvage as much of my Sunday as possible."

I glance over my shoulder just in time to see Nick give Gypsy one of the treats I have been keeping in the pantry and giving her a scratch behind her ears.

Did you hear that?

It was men and women all over the world, swooning in unison.

"Come on, St. Nick, let's do this."

I head outside, pulling my jacket tighter around me the moment I walk out into the freezing morning, and consider how I'm going to get through today.

I was sure Nick was going to make a move last night, but when I came back downstairs, the moment seemed to have disappeared, and instead the only action was on-screen.

To say I'm confused is an understatement. I know I'm not imagining the chemistry between us, so I have to assume my brother is the issue.

If it was up to me, Brandon would have no say in who I date, but I guess I have to admit it could complicate his friendship with Nick. If that's not a risk he's willing to take, then I have to respect that.

Not happily, though.

The truck beeps as Nick unlocks it and I climb into the cab. He slides behind the wheel, turns on the engine and promptly starts playing around with his phone. He turns to me with a shit-eating grin just as Mariah Carey's "All I Want For Christmas" starts blaring through the speakers.

"Oh my god." I smack a hand at his stereo system, turning the volume down—waaaay down—before leveling him with my most cutting look. "That song is the work of the devil and I would appreciate it if you never play it in my presence again."

He laughs so hard he literally has to hold himself upright, so I fold my arms across my chest and wait for him to calm down.

"Fine, fine, fine," he mutters between laughs, his fingers working his phone until the car fills with the soft sounds of "Jingle Bells."

"I guess that's slightly better," I concede, already planning on stealing control of the music as soon as possible. If today doesn't call for a little Beyonce, I don't know what does.

"You want some candy?" I reach into my purse and start rummaging around.

"What've you got?"

"Umm…" *Where are they?* I really need a smaller purse. "Aha!" I pull out a handful of candy canes and York patties and shove them in his direction.

It takes him a moment to respond, and in that time I get the distinct impression he's trying not to laugh at me again.

"You want one or not?"

"Sure, I'll take a candy cane."

I unwrap one and hand it to him before opening a pattie and popping it in my mouth.

"How was Troy when he picked up Tahlia?"

"He's fine, turns out it's just a twisted ankle so nothing serious. He's sorry he missed you." Which is true. I may have mentioned Nick to him a few—million —times, and he's dying for them to meet, so he was disappointed to find Nick was out on a run when he and Matthew arrived. They stuck around as long as possible but Tahlia's demands to get home to her pet guinea pig finally won out.

Sidenote, what sort of psycho *runs* in weather like this? It's probably for the best that nothing happens between us, because that sort of incompatibility is hard to overcome.

"Yeah, me too. I didn't think they would come so early."

"Oh, please," I snort. "I'm surprised they weren't at the door in the middle of the night to take her home. They're kind of helicopter parents." I make a face at him. "But don't ever say that to them, they'll deny it until their dying day."

"Noted." His fingers tap on the steering wheel, keeping time to the music. His fingers are long and thick and... distracting.

Now that I think about it, his hands are really quite nice too. Large and slightly calloused, they're very capable-looking. Like they know how to handle a piece of wood.

I choke on that thought, as well as the chocolate in my mouth, and gasp out a cough.

"Are you okay?" Nick reaches out a hand and pats me gently on the back until I stop coughing. It takes longer than it should since the feel of his hand on my back only serves to remind me of the thought that started this in the first place.

I meant *wood*, wood, not *penis* wood.

I am almost ninety-seven percent sure that's what I meant.

"How did you and Troy meet anyway? He's older than you, right?"

"Yep, he's practically ancient." I throw him a nervous look. "Again, don't tell him I said that. He's a little sensitive about his age since he turned thirty-five."

"I'll be sure to keep that to myself next time Troy and I are having a heart-to-heart." His lips quirk, trying to hold back a smile, but I'm too preoccupied by the golden scruff covering his strong jaw to really pay attention to his teasing. His dark blond hair is messy, as though all he did was run his hands through it after showering, and his jade green eyes are narrowed and focused on the road in front of us.

"Right." I force a laugh and try to stop fixating on everything I shouldn't be thinking about. "Anyway, he's the creative director at *Avondale*, he oversees all the graphic designers, and when I started interning the summer before college, he was my coordinator. I know it seems crazy, considering I was an eighteen-year-old college student, and he was a twenty-nine-year-old married, father-to-be, but we just hit it off right away. We're pretty similar, despite the age difference. We have the same sense of humor, the same morals. We're both passionate about our families and our work." I shrug. "Their surrogate got pregnant not long after we met, so I've been around Tahlia's entire life. That little girl has both Troy and Matthew wrapped around her little finger. It's scary at times, and I'm fairly certain she's going to rule the world one day."

"I can see that, for sure." His voice is softer than usual and it reminds me of the way he spoke to Tahlia yesterday.

"What about you?"

"What about me?"

"Who are your people? I mean besides Brandon and Cohen." I tell myself I'm just making conversation. That the last two nights haven't inspired a need to know everything about him.

His jaw clenches and it takes him a beat too long to answer.

"There's not many. I lost touch with most people from

high school when I moved to Washington for college. After I lost Dad, I was written off by pretty much everyone there when they got tired of putting up with my shit. After I lost my job, I decided to cut my losses and move back home." He cuts his eyes to me and I detest the unhappiness I see in them. "I wish I could say I came back for more honorable reasons, but I really just wanted somewhere to crash while I drank my life away." He white-knuckles the steering wheel. "That was really my only plan back then."

"What changed?"

"What changed? Someone told me to take my head out of my ass and get my shit together. It seemed like good advice, so I gave it a go."

"Well, she sounds delightfully astute." I try to keep my tone playful but I can't deny it feels good to know our conversation had an impact on him. I remember those days vividly, the worry Brandon felt for his best friend and the strain it was putting him under. I honestly can't even fathom what Nick was going through. If we lost my dad, I... I can't even think about what I would do.

"Seriously, I'm glad I helped, but I'm sure there was more to it than that."

"Yeah..." He trails off, swallowing hard and then clearing his throat. "My mom pulled me up on my shit. I got in at some ungodly hour one morning and she was waiting up for me. Her face was all red, like it had been scrubbed raw and her eyes were glassy, but she wasn't crying." His voice is rough and forced and I know this is hard for him. I want to offer him support so I do the only thing I can think of and place a hand on his knee, squeezing lightly.

His eyes drift to my hand resting there, but he says nothing about it, he simply continues his story.

"She told me she couldn't watch me destroy myself, that she loved me too much to do it and I had two choices. Go and talk to someone about losing Dad and show her I was making a real effort to get my life together. Or get out." His mouth tips in a half-smile. "I had never seen my mother like that before and it scared the shit out of me. I had just lost Dad and I couldn't risk losing her too. So I started seeing a psychologist once a week and cut back on the drinking. I got a job in construction, doing pretty much what I was doing back in Washington. But I needed a distraction when I wasn't working, so I started building stuff. Small things at first, but then I built a dining table for Mom and a friend of hers loved it and asked me to build her a TV unit."

"And that's how your business started?"

"Pretty much. One job led to another, and suddenly I had enough business to leave the construction job. Cohen helps me out with the business side of things, and Brandon and Amy are always recommending me to people. So, yeah, my circle is small, but it's strong and I'm grateful for each of them."

"I'm really happy for you, Nick. You deserve to be happy. I hope you know how proud your dad would be. And. God, starting your own business. I don't think I could ever do that, I'm not brave enough."

"I think you're plenty brave." He clears his throat

again but keeps his eyes straight ahead. "But it seemed right. I think I was always a bit envious of your family growing up, and the family business was a part of that. Your parents worked just as hard as mine, but it felt more grounded in family, you know? Because it was all going to be yours one day, if you wanted it. I like the idea of that. Building something that my kids can have."

I break out in a small sweat at the idea of Nick with kids, but force myself to ignore the image.

Images.

So many images.

Nick holding a sleeping baby.

Nick tucking a sleepy toddler into bed.

Nick holding a tiny hand in his own large one.

Removing my hand from Nick's knee, I rub both hands across my eyes, trying to shake the pictures loose.

"It's definitely different when the business is yours. Brandon and I practically lived there growing up. Mom technically worked part-time after we were born, but she and Dad built the company up together, so it's in her blood just as much as his. It was kind of instilled in us that the business was a part of our family, and Brandon and I grew to love it as much as Mom and Dad did."

"Brandon was always so sure that he wanted to work there, and I guess you were too?" He cuts his eyes to me, looking for confirmation.

"Yeah, it seemed inevitable. We were lucky enough

to spend time in each department and get a feel for where we fit," I muse. "God, we really were so lucky."

"You know, I always wondered… the name. Where did *Avondale* come from?"

"Oh, that's where my parents are from. It's a tiny town in Minnesota. They moved to New York after college, but they missed home, so when they set up the business and decided to focus on greeting cards, *Greetings from Avondale* just made sense. It was their way of honoring their family, I guess."

"Your parents are good people."

"Yeah, they are. So are yours." I shrug. "They're just diff—what? What's that look?"

He turns to me and straight away I think of the expression Tahlia has when she's up to no good.

"We're here."

8

NICK

As if in slow motion, she turns and takes in the huge, almost empty lot to our right. In a matter of seconds, about twenty different emotions are reflected in those gorgeous eyes.

She settles on disbelief.

"Christmas trees?"

"Yep." I indicate and make the turn into the lot.

"What sort of tree do you think you're going to get a week before Christmas?"

"I think *we* are going to find just the tree we need."

Relieved that we have finally made it, I park quickly and practically vault out of the car. I underestimated how tough it would be in such a confined space with her. For someone who hates Christmas so damn much, she smells like a walking advertisement for it. Peppermint, chocolate, and today there's a hint of cinnamon. She's got me goddamn salivating.

I know what you're thinking. I was going to make my move last night.

And you'd be right.

I one hundred percent pussied out.

But tonight is the night. I figure after a day of Christmas spirit, I'll cook her a nice meal—my world-famous mac and cheese, thank you very much—and then… well, I can't give away all my secrets now, can I?

I'm feeling good about my plan. Once I win her over to Christmas, I'll win her over to me.

I'm practically a genius.

A car door slams behind me, and I hear her run to catch up. I steel myself to be overwhelmed by her scent. I swear to God, just the sight of a candy cane is enough to give me a hard-on these days.

"Christmas is in exactly seven days, all they're going to have left are the pitiful, rejected trees."

"Anything can be made beautiful with a bit of Christmas spirit." I pause. "And some tinsel." I run an eye along the line of trees available to buy and mutter, "A lot of tinsel."

We spend the next hour trawling through the trees until we settle on a smallish tree that looks like it has the best chance of surviving through to Christmas Day.

"We'll take the tree out back and net it for you. My wife is at the front of the lot and she'll take payment. We'll meet you in the parking lot to help you load it on your car."

We thank the owner and his assistant for their help and make our way to find his wife.

"That was fun, right? It's not really Christmas until you have a tree and I think that's going to be a beauty."

She looks at me as if I'm crazy but simply nods her head and mumbles a noncommittal, "Mmm."

"How are you folks this morning? I'm Flora, Ned's wife."

"Nice to meet you, ma'am." Holly offers her hand and Flora takes it warmly.

"Okay, let's get you kids sorted out so you can be on your way." Her smile is warm and she gives off grandma vibes that I'm sure are good for business.

I hand over the money for the tree and Flora is passing me my change when she glances up above our heads.

Pointing in the same direction, she asks, "Would you look at that?"

We follow her finger to find we're standing underneath lights that are strung up all around the perimeter of the lot. Easy to miss during the day when they're not lit up.

Also randomly hung up is an occasional sprig of mistletoe, one of which Holly and I happen to be standing right underneath.

"Look at you lovebirds, under the mistletoe." She turns to me with a wink. "You best kiss your lady, young man."

I can't explain what happens next.

I should have returned her kind smile and explained we weren't a couple.

Instead, I find myself bending down to brush a kiss across Holly's pink lips, bracing myself for what is about to happen.

It was supposed to be a chaste kiss. A simple touch

to appease an old lady. But as soon as I make contact, everything shifts and the simple touch turns into a burning need that succeeds in alleviating nothing.

My hand finds its way to her cheek as my tongue licks along the seam of her lips. She opens for me and the moment my tongue slides against hers, tasting her after years of need, I step into her and bring her body flush with mine.

Her long hair tangles in my fingers and when her hands settle on the waistband of my jeans, her fingertips brushing along my skin, a groan that has belonged to her for the last three years, bursts free.

An embarrassed cough drags us out of whatever spell we are under, and we pull apart abruptly. Holly's face is flushed and her eyes seem startled, but she doesn't break my gaze. She meets my eye, almost as if in challenge.

"Oh my, young love," Flora coos, a hand held to her heart. "I remember it well."

Still, neither of us offer the denial we should. Instead letting the lie linger in the air as though daring us to expose ourselves.

It's going to be a long drive home.

We pull into the driveway an hour later and I shut off the engine, but I don't make a move to get out of the car.

The ride home was torturously long with neither of us prepared to break the silence.

The silence which wasn't uncomfortable exactly. It was more...

Anticipatory.

We sit there for a moment until I can't take it any longer.

"Inside. Now." I wrench the door open and storm to the house, never doubting that Holly will be right behind me.

Getting the key in the lock proves to be harder than it should, but when I finally succeed, I fling the door open and welcome the sound it makes when it slams into the wall.

It echoes the slamming of my heart in my chest.

I smell her before I see her.

Fucking peppermint.

Without thinking about what I'm about to do, I spin around and pull her to me. Slamming the door, I push her back until she crashes into it and I press against her, not stopping until every inch of her body is covered by me.

She's fucking intoxicating. I run my nose along the column of her neck and have to stop myself from biting along her pulse point. Instead I still, and take a moment to enjoy the way it's thrashing beneath her creamy skin.

Her breathing is erratic, her eyes closed, and I don't think I have ever felt this powerful and powerless at the same time. This woman could be my downfall. If I don't stop acting on my feelings, an important part of my life could implode.

But stopping isn't an option. It's not even a question of what I want.

It's need.

Visceral. Raw. *Need.*

"Look at me." The second it takes for her eyes to open feels endless. "Tell me to stop." Because she's the only reason I ever would.

"No." Her answer is immediate and holds a challenge.

I lean down and slant my mouth over hers, loving the way she opens for me. As soon as I taste her, my cock kicks against my zipper, so I lower my hands to her ass and grab hold, lifting her and wrapping her legs around my waist.

She rolls her hips against me, causing me to harden even more, and takes control of the kiss. She sucks. Bites. Licks. She destroys what little control I have left and I love it.

My mind plays through every fantasy I've had over the last three years, every dirty thing I've wanted to do to her, and I could laugh at how inadequate my imagination was.

Because the reality of Holly is beyond compare.

"Where?" she gasps, the words falling out on a moan.

"Where what?" My words are muffled against the curve of her neck, which proved too tempting, the perfect canvas for my mark.

"I swear to God, Nick, if you're not inside me in the next sixty seconds I will hate Christmas forever, on principle alone." Her hands fall from my shoulders to my jeans and begin working my zip down, making it clear just how serious she is.

"Jesus," I groan as her hand wraps around my dick and squeezes just hard enough to cause a short-term malfunction in my brain.

Okay, think, O'Connor, *think*.

Where's the nearest surface?

The stairs are the obvious answer. Fine for me, probably not so much for Holly.

"Ugh, Nick!" She pushes hard against my chest, forcing me back a step, and disentangles herself from my grip. "Would you just get naked already."

She emphasizes this by ripping her jacket off and following it with her sweater until she's standing in front of me in only her leggings and a hot-pink bra.

"You know, I'm beginning to think you really don't care about my love of Christmas at all."

I drag my eyes from her tits—because they deserve my attention—and bite back a laugh.

I really fucking like this girl.

"Pants, Nicholas." A frustrated hand is waved in the direction of my dick.

"Yes, ma'am." Coming to my senses, I have my boots, socks, jeans, and shirt off before Holly has even removed her shoes.

I stand there, cock tenting my boxer briefs, and watch her slow, deliberate movements, my frustration growing.

"Holly," I growl.

She quirks an eyebrow my way. "Just a little tit for

tat. There's such a thing as too much anticipation, you know."

She's right. I've suffered through three years of it and enough is enough. I lower my boxers and kick them to the side. "All right. Here's my tat, now let's see your tits."

The smile falls from her lips and she swallows —hard.

She mumbles something under her breath that I don't quite catch—something about sixteen years?—and in a blink and I miss it move, her leggings and panties have been tossed alongside my clothes and she's undoing her bra while stalking toward me.

The bra falls to the ground, and we stand there, staring at each other. My eyes travel the expanse of flawless skin until I can't stand it anymore. I wrap a hand around the back of her neck and draw her to me, my mouth finding hers in a kiss that kills me in the sweetest possible death.

"Sofa," she whispers, breaking our connection and taking hold of my hand.

I follow her into the living room, my eyes glued to her ass as it jiggles with each step, and I have to stop myself from falling to my knees to take a bite out of it.

We reach the couch and I take her mouth again, my hands skating along her curves, taking the time to enjoy how good she feels.

With a cunning I didn't realize I possess, I maneuver us onto the couch, so Holly is straddling me. She pulls back breathlessly, her attention falling to my cock, which she begins to stroke before meeting my eye.

"I've wanted this for a long time, Nick, and I want to take real good care of this guy." She strokes upward to accentuate her point. "But if you get weird after, I'm going to make sure he's out of action for a while, 'kay?"

I want to agree and assure her that she has nothing to worry about, but her hand is on my dick and I'm finding it real hard to talk. All I can do is mumble something incoherent and I hope she understands.

She slides my cock along her slit and teases her clit with it, so I'm going to assume we're good.

"Stop messing around and sit on it, Hols, because I guarantee you I've been waiting for this longer." I reach up and run my thumb over her nipple, smirking as it hardens under my touch. "Mmkay?" I echo her tone from a moment ago.

"Smart-ass," she mutters. But she does as she's told and guides my cock to her entrance, sliding down, taking me inch by inch.

My head falls to her shoulder and I hiss out a slow breath. Nothing will ever feel better than being inside her.

Holly's nails dig into my shoulders and she begins to move, rolling her hips in a slow, smooth motion that has me wanting to slam up into her. I let her set the pace, but every soft moan that falls from her lips has me choking on the need to come. Leaning forward, I take her nipple in my mouth and slip a hand between us, my thumb mirroring the movements of my tongue until I feel her pussy tighten around me, and her movements lose any kind of rhythm.

She comes loudly, pushing my hand away and mumbling, "Too much, too much." When she has finished riding out her orgasm, I grab a handful of ass and thrust up into her until I come with a primal roar.

Holly slumps forward, burrowing her head into my neck.

"Okay, so maybe Christmas isn't *so* bad."

"Now that's a use for tinsel I can get behind." Holly snickers as I untie the golden strand from her wrists. Rolling over, she curls into my side and runs her fingernails over my chest. The last few hours have been split between decorating the Christmas tree and seeing how many times I can make her come.

We're at three, if anyone is curious.

"What did you mean when you said you'd been wanting this longer than me?"

I watch her fingers trace patterns over my chest and try to figure out the best way to admit I've been wanting her for years. Is there a way to say that without sounding like a creeper?

I'm about to open my mouth and confess it all when my phone starts buzzing from across the room.

"Hold that thought, it might be my super, I've been trying to get in touch with him since yesterday."

I get up and grab my jeans, pulling my phone out of

the pocket. Dread washes over me when I see the name on the screen.

"What's wrong?" Holly rolls over, pulling the blanket we have been using as a makeshift bed up to cover her.

"It's Brandon."

"What did he want?" Billie grabs her sandwich from the break room fridge and slides into the chair next to mine.

"He was just checking in, I think. I couldn't really tell much from Nick's side of the conversation."

"He didn't tell you what Brandon wanted?" Troy doesn't even bother to hide his surprise.

"There wasn't anything to tell. They only spoke for a couple of minutes." I ignore the ache in my stomach when I recall Nick's words.

"No, I haven't seen her since Friday night."

It was a bald-faced lie. But it was one we had both readily agreed on, already deciding that we would wait to tell Brandon until he arrived home.

So why does the way the lie slipped so easily from his tongue make me so anxious.

"What does this mean?" Billie prods. "Are you dating? Fucking? What?"

"Dating. Definitely dating. We both want to see

where this could go." I reach over and snatch a cranberry from Troy's salad.

"If it helps, Tahlia might be slightly in love with him. She couldn't stop talking about him yesterday." Troy's brow is furrowed. "It was both endearing and terrifying at the same time."

"Well, if Holly's anything to go by, get used to it. She —" Billie waves a hand my way. "Hasn't shut up about him since I met her."

"Please," I scoff. "That is absolutely not true."

Billie's mouth drops open. "It absolutely *is* true." She stops, narrowing her eyes at me. "Do you not realize you're doing it?"

"Do what?" I don't know what she's talking about. After Nick left for college, I didn't even see him for five years and I can count on one hand the number of times I've seen him since he moved back home.

There is no way I have mentioned him more than a few times in passing.

No way.

"You talk about him all the time, Hols." Troy backs up Billie and obviously our friendship is over. "Just last week I was telling you about my cousin's wedding in Baltimore and you told me about some random football game he played there his freshman year of college."

"It was his first game and his parents couldn't go, so Brandon and I went instead." I sound defensive even to my own ears.

Billie puts her half-eaten sandwich down and leans toward me. "I think we're just saying that maybe your feelings are stronger than you realize and we want you to be careful."

"Right," Troy agrees. "His friendship with your brother makes this a tricky situation and we don't want you to get hurt. You both need to be sure of your feelings if you're going to take the risk of alienating Brandon."

"You don't need to worry," I assure them. "We both know what we're doing and trust me, Brandon wants both of us to be happy. If that means Nick and I being together, then he won't have a problem with it."

Right?

Ignoring the cold, I put my head down and power through the biting wind as I make my way into the movie theater. Nick better have a good reason for dragging me out tonight.

It has been a long day full of work that wouldn't come together and a lot of second-guessing everything that happened yesterday. Not helping was the fact that I didn't hear a word from Nick until right before I finished work.

Even then, all I got was one line of text.

Meet me at the Regal on 42nd Street in half an hour.

Despite my exhaustion, excitement at seeing him had me rushing down to grab a cab for the short trip to the theater.

It's colder than I expected and I realize I left my

jacket back at the office, so I wrap my arms around my waist, shocked at how chilled the thirty-second walk from the curb to inside the building has left me.

As soon as I step inside, I hear my name called and look up to find Nick sauntering toward me. The minute I see his face all my doubts evaporate and I remember the most important thing he said to me yesterday.

"I'm in this, Holly. We're not going to sneak around or lie to Brandon a second longer than we have to. We'll tell him as soon as he gets home."

And I choose to believe him.

"Hi," I murmur as he reaches me, bending down to brush a kiss along my mouth. He follows it with a brief touch of his lips to the slope of my neck that sends goose bumps shooting along my skin.

"We're seeing a movie?"

"Movies." He accentuates the S and it's then that I look up and see all the signs advertising tonight's movie marathon.

Tonight's *Christmas* movie marathon.

"Oh. How... festive."

He laughs and hands me a tub of popcorn I hadn't noticed he was holding. "Extra butter, right?"

I nod, a small smile tilting the corners of my lips.

"Trust me, if you're not feeling the Christmas spirit after these movies, you just might be broken beyond repair."

I snort and try to hide my amusement. Does he really think I haven't already seen every Christmas movie ever made over the years?

But I love his determination, and I'm not about to be the one to dash his hopes.

"Okay, what's on the agenda." I glance up at the sign again and check out the listing. *Home Alone, Elf* and *Die Hard.*"Wait, *Die Hard? Die Hard is not a Christmas movie.*"

"Careful, Hols, this could very well be our first fight as a couple." His hand falls to my lower back and he begins to guide me toward the theater. The combination of his touch and him calling us a couple has my brain going fuzzy for a second.

"I guess I wouldn't want that. All right, you have sixty seconds to present your case. Go." I shove a handful of popcorn into my mouth and wait.

"I don't need sixty seconds, babe. Ignore the obvious reasons like it's set on Christmas Eve, there's Christmas music and a shitload of Christmas references. At its core, it's a movie about family and how far a person will go, what they'll risk, for the people they love." He grins at me. "Also, Stephen de Souza said it is, so it's really not even up for debate."

"Who is... you know what? I don't care. That was a very succinct, well-formed argument. I give it a B+. You're still wrong, but I appreciate your effort." I reach up on my tiptoes and place a kiss on his scruffy cheek.

"You know what? We'll revisit this after because I think you'll be convinced by the time we walk out of here."

"If you say so." I don't bother to hide my disbelief.

"Are you hungry? I know you came straight from work, do you want me to grab some pizza from the concession stand now or later?"

I slip my arm around his waist and snuggle in, resting my head on his chest. "Later is good. Let's get in there and snag a back-row seat so we can make out anytime the word Christmas is mentioned."

His arm falls from my shoulders and he grabs my hand, immediately dragging me toward the theater. "Yeah, your plan is much better than mine."

୧ଈ

The cab flies through the deserted streets and I already know I'm going to be a wreck tomorrow—or should I say today—at work, but I can't regret a moment of it. And, I'm not quite ready to admit it, but watching those movies beside a man who fills me with warmth and optimism, in a theater filled with laughter and happiness, it did move something in me. An emotion I can't quite put words to. But I like it.

The slight jarring of motion has my eyes blinking sleepily until I can't keep them open. Nick's beside me, silently watching the world pass by in a blur of motion. He has me wrapped up tightly, pulled into his side, giving me the peace of mind that allows sleep to overtake me.

I am drifting along the edge of consciousness when I hear Nick's whispered words, but I'm too far gone to pry my eyes open.

Later, I'll wonder if I dreamed it. If it was a figment of my overactive imagination. But as I fall into slumber, I do so, safe in the knowledge that Nick loves me.

NICK

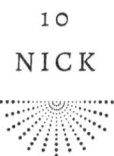

I told her I love her.

She was unconscious at the time but, still.

Way to scare her off, O'Connor.

I clamp a beautiful piece of white oak to my workbench and try to get my head in the game. Being distracted while using power tools is a surefire way to lose a finger, and Holly seemed to rather enjoy my fingers the other day, so I would like to keep them all.

I grab the tape measure and a pencil, ready to start marking up measurements when there's a loud knock on the open roller door.

Turning around, I spot Lincoln standing there, a bag of food in hand and an easy grin on his face.

Lincoln McCade and his brother, Harrison, rent the workspace next door to me. While mine is set up as a builder's workshop, theirs is a tech-head's delight, where they run their cybersecurity business.

We have become good friends over the last couple

of years, and I'm ashamed to realize it's been a week since I last saw him.

"Hey man, where have you been?"

"Denver, had to put together a presentation for a law firm over there." He holds up the bag and my stomach rumbles in response. "Tacos from the food truck."

"I could kiss you, I skipped breakfast." I grab some sodas from the fridge and we sit on the deck chairs.

"Dude, you gotta get some better chairs, these ones kill my ass," Linc gripes.

"I know," I mumble around a mouthful of food, knowing full well I won't do anything about them. "How's things? How's your girl?"

"We broke up." He picks up his drink and gulps down half the can before digging back into his taco.

"You seem devastated," I observe wryly.

He shrugs noncommittally. "We weren't serious."

"So why'd you break up?" I really am curious. Linc's relationships never last long and he ends things for the most ridiculous reasons.

"She used too many emojis."

My taco stops halfway to my mouth and I let it hang there while I try to make sense of what he just said. "Too many emojis?"

"Yeah, like she ended every message with about twenty emojis. Sometimes it would be an entire message of emojis. It was too much."

I shake my head slowly, watching him closely. "You know that's messed up, right?"

"Yeah," he sighs, finishing off his last bite. "She just wasn't the one."

"God, you are such a Chandler," I mumble under my breath.

"What?"

"Nothing. Listen, how are you going to find the one if you keep breaking up with women over stupid shit like that?"

He crumples his trash and tosses it into the trash can. "It's complicated. And not worth talking about. What about you? Did you get that coffee table finished last week?"

"Yeah, I even got it delivered a day early. It's been a good week." I give him a quick rundown of everything that has happened since last week.

"I can't believe you finally did it. I thought you were too scared of Brandon to ever make a move on her."

"Hold up." I hold a hand up in denial. "I am not scared of Brandon. I was being a good guy and putting our friendship first."

"And now you're not a good guy?" He snorts. "I don't care why you finally did something about it, I'm just glad you did." Linc sobers suddenly. "Friendship is great, but love is better. It's what gives us purpose and if you have the chance to actually be with the person you love and you didn't take it, I would judge you pretty damn hard."

There's a story there, I'm sure of it, but Lincoln quickly changes the subject, making it clear that he's done talking about it.

Later, when he's gone, I consider his words and

realize how right he is. I love Brandon and if this ends our friendship it will suck, but what's happening between Holly and me feels inevitable.

We have chemistry that can't be ignored and a foundation of friendship and history that together creates something exceptional.

I won't lose that for any reason.

I won't lose *her*.

The parking lot is almost full when I pull into it and it takes a while to find an empty space. Cursing myself for not leaving work earlier, I'm about to get out of the car and head into the supermarket when my phone goes off. Happy to delay the inevitable crowd I'm about to face, I pull it out of my pocket.

"For fuck's sake," I groan. I don't know what the hell is going on with Brandon's sudden affinity for phone calls, but I really miss the days where we only communicated through text.

Lying that way inspires a lot less guilt.

"What's up, B? I'm about to run into the grocery store, so can we make this quick?"

"Since when do you go to grocery stores? I thought you got everything delivered?"

I picture the look on his face, knowing how much shit he gives me because I hate picking up groceries.

"It's just a few things I forgot to order. What do you need?"

"Okay, okay, I can take a hint. I just wanted to see how things are going at the house."

"You remember calling a few days ago, right? Not much has changed since then." I scrub a hand over my jaw and make a note to shave tomorrow.

"Sure, what about Holly? Is everything okay with her?"

For a moment I worry that he knows, but that's ridiculous. There is no way it's possible.

"She's fine, I guess. I haven't seen much of her." The lie tastes bitter on my tongue.

"Really? I was hoping you would keep her company. You know what she's like this time of year." His voice is full of reproach and I worry that I've been too convincing in my apathy.

"We had dinner together last night and she seems good. She was talking about some book club she has tomorrow night. I don't think you need to worry about her, B," I try to reassure him.

"Okay, that's good to hear. Any idea when you can get back to your apartment?"

"No." I sigh. "Max, my super called not long after I spoke to you on Sunday and said they had run into some trouble with the pipes, so it would be another couple of days. I've been trying to get hold of him today, but haven't had any luck." I don't mention that I'm not trying too hard, more than happy to stay right where I am for the time being.

"Huh, I'm sure you'll hear from him soon. Anyway, I'll let you go do your shopping. Just keep an eye on Holly, okay? It'll give me some peace of mind."

"Of course I will."

After I've hung up, I sit there for a moment trying to figure out what I'm feeling. There's definitely some guilt over the lying. But stronger than that is the feeling that we're doing the right thing.

Holly and I need to tell him face-to-face, not over the phone.

Confident once again in the decisions we have made, I jump out of my truck and head inside to face the crowds.

It's time to put step three of *'Get Holly in the Christmas Spirit'* into action.

"Why does yours look so much better than mine?"

I take a step back and look at our gingerbread houses side by side, trying to resist the urge to gloat.

Because, yeah, mine kicks ass.

"What did you use for the shingles on the roof?" There is a tiny little crease between her eyebrows as she frowns down at my house.

"Sliced almonds."

"Where did you get them?" she shrieks, waving an indignant finger at my roof.

"They're right there," I reply sardonically, pointing to the pile of junk I bought for us to decorate the pre-made houses.

"Oh." She folds her lips between her teeth and crosses her arms over her chest, just staring at our creations. "Okay, I'm going to need you to pretend this never happened."

"Not a chance in hell, I killed it. I say we take photos to document my victory." I pull my phone out and start to snap away when I notice something missing. "What happened to your candy canes? I saw you take a bunch."

"I ate them." She shrugs unapologetically.

I swipe all the leftover food into the shopping bag and when Holly's not looking, I toss Gypsy, who is asleep under the dining table, one of her dog treats, that I've taken to carrying in my pocket. She opens her eyes when she hears the treat land, gobbles it up and goes straight back to sleep.

"You really like the whole peppermint thing, don't you?" Not that I'm complaining.

"I guess." She moves the gingerbread houses over to the kitchen island and comes back to help me clean up. "When I was little my parents would spend the twenty-third preparing for their Christmas party, so they would send Brandon to our nana and papa's and I would go to our great-grandma's for the day. It was my favorite day of the year. She used to take me shopping for a birthday present at this tiny little toy store that was around the corner from her apartment." Her face takes on this faraway quality and I sneak a photo of her. "I would spend hours in that shop and Grandma Ginny never rushed me. She would slip me candy canes all day and basically let me do whatever I wanted. December twenty-third was my day of magic and I looked forward to it all year." She bites her lip and starts hurrying to put the rest of the things away, turning away from me. "Ginny passed away when I was seven. Peppermint reminds me of her. I have peppermint scented shampoo, moisturizer, hand cream, everything. I probably go overboard, but—" Holly shakes her head and she gives in to a small smile. "She deserves to be remembered."

I cross the room and wrap her in a hug, kissing the top of her head.

"I like your heart, you know that? It's pretty damn special."

She pulls back slightly, looking up at me before she opens her mouth as if to say something.

Instead, she lets her head fall to my chest and I hear her whisper, "I like your heart, too."

"Who's coming again?"

Nick sits on the floor, throwing a ball for Gypsy and watching me finish loading the coffee table with snacks.

"Billie, April, and Owen. Oh, and Tessa will be Face-Timing with us from whatever city she's in at the moment."

"And, you work with Billie, April and Tessa, right? How do you know Owen?"

"Owen is married to Tessa's college roommate. She set them up and they are the reason Tessie now thinks she's god's gift to matchmaking. If anyone ever tries to refuse a setup, the first thing out of her mouth is, *'But you've heard about Carrie and Owen, right?'*" I roll my eyes. "Apparently getting it right once entitles her to fix up every single person she comes across."

I head back to the kitchen to grab the charcuterie board I made earlier. Nick hops up and follows me, and

I pretend not to notice the handful of pretzels that he grabs.

"They're her only success story?" he prods.

"Uh…" I give the platter a final once-over. "No, I actually think she has a pretty good track record. With people who want to be set up, that is."

"What do you mean?" I see him give Gypsy a pretzel from the corner of my eye.

"Don't give her people food, Nick!"

I scowl at him across the room and he throws his hands up before sauntering over to me. "Sorry." He kisses my shoulder and then reaches down for a cube of cheese.

I am going to kill him if he doesn't leave soon.

"I mean, who has she tried to set up who didn't want to be?"

"Billie." I snort out a laugh, thinking about all of Tessa's failed matchmaking attempts with Billie and the parade of different men. "She's been trying to set her up for at least six months."

"Ah." He wraps his arms around my middle and leans his chin on my shoulder. "I thought you were going to say you."

A shiver skates up my spine at the feel of his warm breath on my skin and the memory of a long-forgotten conversation with Tessa flashes through my mind.

"Why have you never tried to set me up?" I wring my hands awkwardly. I mean, it's not that I want to be set up, but, also, it's kind of embarrassing that she's never tried. I'm a catch, dammit!

"Oh, honey." She pats my shoulder sympathetically.

"You're in love with your brother's friend. There would be no point in setting you up with someone."

Yeah, he doesn't need to know that.

"Nope, I told her I wasn't interested and she respected that. Um, what are you doing tonight?" I fumble to change the subject before he notices the contradiction in what I just told him. "You don't need to leave, you know. Nobody will mind if you're lurking around."

"As much as I would love to be a lurker, I've made plans with Cohen. You're still not working tomorrow, right?"

"No, *Avondale* closes from the twenty-third until the sixth. My only plans for tomorrow are sleeping in and then packing to go home." I turn in his arms so we're face-to-face. "We should talk about what we're going to say to Brandon tomorrow, right? I think he said they're going to leave Philly in the afternoon. Amy has tickets for *The Nutcracker* tomorrow night."

"How the hell did she get Brandon to agree to that?" I laugh.

"I don't want to know." I pull a face. "Maybe we can have breakfast before you go to work and discuss it?"

"I'm taking tomorrow off." He leans down and kisses my forehead. "I'm not working on anything urgent, so I thought we could spend the day together."

Nodding, I bite back a smile. "That sounds nice." He nuzzles down into my neck, and I curse out loud when the doorbell sounds just as his teeth find my earlobe.

"That's my cue." He chuckles, pushing away from me. "I'll let whoever it is in and I'll see you tonight." He comes back for one last kiss but before I get the chance to deepen it, he pulls away and is gone.

❦

"I definitely see what you're saying, Owen," April agrees. "I think the bully trope is a hard one for men to understand because it goes against everything you've ever been told."

"Right. I was reading it, thinking why didn't she just punch him in the junk and tell him to fuck off?" He throws back a handful of cashews. "I'm pretty sure that's what Carrie would do to me if I tried to pull any of that shit."

"It's the fantasy of it, though." Tessa's face peers out at us from the laptop screen. "You're right, if a guy was ever as much of a dick to me in real life as Vicious is to Emilia, I would want nothing to do with him. Truth be told, and this is no offense to the male population as a whole, Owen, the majority of you are quite decent human beings, but most women have come across enough dickheads that we have a top ten list."

"Hear hear!" Billie holds her soda up in a mock salute causing Tessa to giggle and April to roll her eyes.

"I just think that there is something kind of empowering in being the one to tame—for lack of a better word—an asshole. Vicious is as much of a bastard at the end of the book as he is at the start, except with Emilia. I think that notion of being the exception for someone is quite intoxicating."

"In fiction," April adds with a wry smile as we all take in Tessa's dreamy expression.

"Well, I love bully romance. Reading about the worst kind of prick being brought to his knees by the woman he loves? I eat that shit up," Billie declares.

"Yeah, I can kind of understand that, I guess. But I don't think the bully thing is really for me. I did enjoy —" He glances down at his paperback. "LJ Shen's writing style, I found it pretty addictive, so I'm happy for us to keep reading the series."

Billie, Tessa, and April agree and I practically bounce in my seat with excitement.

"Good, because Dean and Rosie are next and, ugh, they are going to rip your heart apart."

"Christ, Hols," April grumbles. "You're a little too excited about our emotional destruction."

"Yes." I rub my hands together gleefully. "Yes, I am."

"All right, well, thanks for tonight ladies, but I'm going to head out. I promised Carrie I would pick her up a pint of cookie dough ice cream on my way home."

"Ooooh, craving?" April asks.

"Yeah, she's going through a pint a day since she hit the third trimester. I'm thinking about buying shares in Ben & Jerry's."

"Having a baby must be so weird," she counters. "It's like you have no control over your body, you hand it all over to a tiny little alien that has squatter's rights."

"April!" Tessa chides.

"What?" April looks at us wide-eyed until her gaze lands on Owen, when it turns sympathetic. "I mean, it's a *magical* little alien."

"And on that note." Owen starts gathering his things and April quickly follows suit.

"Yeah, I better be on my way too. I have to drive to my sister's tomorrow."

"I'll say goodnight too," Tessa pipes up. "I have an early flight tomorrow."

Twenty minutes later, it's only Billie and I left and we settle back on the sofa with a bowl of Reese's Pieces between us.

"So tomorrows the big day, huh? Do you know how you're going to tell Brandon?"

"No," I sigh. "But I think the best thing is to just sit him down and tell him straight out. No fuss, no muss. I really don't think he'll be upset. Probably shocked, but he'll get over that."

"Yeah, maybe."

"You don't sound convinced." I worry my bottom lip between my teeth.

"Ugh, ignore me, Hols. I'm a pessimistic bitch, you know that." She gives me an unconvincing smile. "You know Brandon better than anyone, even Nick. If you think he'll be fine, then I'm sure he will."

"You know what I really think? I think we need wine."

"Holly? Wake up, baby."

"No, go away," I mumble, burrowing into my pillow.

A hand starts gently sweeping hair off my face but I quickly swat it away and curl into a ball, pulling the covers over my head. It does little to disguise the sound of his laughter.

The next minute I feel a body sneak in under the blanket and wrap itself around me.

"Happy Hollymas," he whispers in my ear, catching my attention.

"What?" I demand, rolling over. "What's Hollymas?" I can already feel a smile trying to break free.

"I know your great-grandma started the tradition, but I'd like to pick up the baton she left. Christmas might have stolen your birthday's thunder but I am officially declaring December twenty-third, Hollymas." Kisses are peppered along my jaw. "The official holiday of Holly Curtis."

Pulling back, I look at him, wondering if he's too good to be true.

"That's crazy." I place a hand on his cheek, letting the stubble tickle my palm. He turns his head slightly until his lips find the sensitive skin.

"No, it's what you deserve. Now..." He reaches down and grabs a handful of my ass and squeezes. Hard. "Get dressed and be in my truck in thirty minutes."

NICK

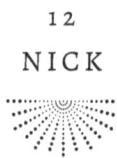

"*T*hat breakfast was amazing."

It turns out the way to Holly's heart is through bacon, waffles, and peppermint hot chocolate. You can bet your ass I've locked that information away for later.

"So, where are we going now?" Her face is glued to the windshield, and I just give her a noncommittal grunt.

"Did you hear from your super yet?"

"No, not yet. But he called after I spoke to Brandon the other night and said I'm good to go back to the apartment tomorrow. Kind of dreading the mess I'm sure I'll be going back to."

"A week is a long time, but I guess the time of year didn't help things." She pulls her purse on her lap and pulls out a couple of candy canes. Unwrapping one, she sticks it in my mouth before claiming the other one. "Did you ever find out what was wrong with the plumbing?"

"He was pretty vague, something about the pipes. To be honest, I didn't really care, I was just trying to figure out what I was going to do."

"It was pretty serendipitous." Turning to me, her face is lit up by a beaming smile. "If your pipes hadn't exploded, or whatever they did, we wouldn't have ended up at the house together and I wouldn't be able to do this." She leans over and kisses my cheek, then nibbles on my earlobe.

"You could say it's Christmas magic."

Her entire face scrunches up. "Too far, Nick. Too far. That was corn with a side of cheese, and you're better than that."

Her laughter fills the car and I have no choice but to turn and look at her. It's almost impossible to keep my eyes off her at the best of times, but when she's like this? It's inconceivable.

Luckily, I turn my attention back to the road just in time to see our final turn, and only minutes later I pull into the parking lot in front of my workshop.

"Where are we?" She spins in her seat, her head swinging back and forth, taking in the row of what looks to be large storage containers.

"This is my workshop." I cut the engine and take off my seat belt. "I need you to wait here for a second, okay?"

"Mmmhmm," she murmurs, her hand already reaching for her own seat belt.

"Holly, I mean it. Give me a few minutes and I'll be right back. But do not come in without me. Got it?"

"Sir, yes, sir." She salutes me.

Fucking impossible woman. I give her nose a kiss and then jump out of my truck.

It takes me a minute to unlock the roller door that is in the middle of the makeshift building and I pull it halfway down again, behind me, so Holly can't see inside. Heading to the left of the workshop, where I do my furniture designs, I cast a quick eye over everything I set up last night. All my equipment is pushed along the walls and it's all neat and tidy. A large blanket with some pillows is laid out on the floor and I quickly turn on the fairy lights I've strung up around the room.

Satisfied, I make my way back to Holly and I'm halfway to the door when I realize I forgot the most important thing. Spinning around, I jog over to my drafting table and pick up the wrapped present, placing it in the middle of the blanket.

I duck under the roller door and almost crash into Holly, who was just about to enter.

"You were taking too long," is her meek explanation.

I shake my head, but take her hand and tell her to shut her eyes. She does but as soon as we walk into the workshop they spring open.

Walking to the right, she pulls out of my reach and goes straight to the wood I have clamped on the bench and runs a hand over it.

"What are you making?"

"It's going to be a hutch. But your surprise is this way."

Holly turns and her hands fly to her mouth. "It's so pretty, Nick." She throws herself into my arms and kisses me, her tongue sliding against mine in a way that has me hardening uncomfortably.

Breaking our connection, I put her down and pull her gently over to the blanket.

"I have things planned for later, but this place is such an important part of my life, and I wanted you to see it, so it seemed like a good place to give you your present." I push the gift her way, wishing I was better at wrapping and it didn't look like I used an entire roll of sticky tape on it. Because I did.

She looks up at me from under her lashes, her lips quirking. "It's not my birthday."

"It's not a birthday present. It's a Hollymas present."

"Well, in that case..." She rips at the wrapping paper, giving me plenty of side-eye. "Have fun with the tape there, did ya?"

My mouth stays shut, because really, what could I say?

Using her nails to rip the tape open and then pulling the paper off in one continuous motion, she stills when she eventually reaches the present.

"Nick..." Her fingers dance across the top of the intricately carved box, tracing the sprigs of holly, while her mouth keeps opening and closing, as if she can't find any words. Finally, she directs her attention my way. "Did you make this? It's so incredibly beautiful."

"I noticed you left your jewelry lying around your room, so I thought you might like a jewelry box. Of course, halfway through, I realized you probably do have one back at your place, but by then I was too far gone to change my mind." I shrug, trying to stop staring at her.

Because that look on her face? I could get addicted to that.

"It's perfect. The best Hollymas present I could have hoped for. I love it." She tears her gaze away from me and I watch closely as she takes in the room once again. "This week has been... I can't believe I'm about to say this, but it's been pretty damn incredible." Grinning, she turns back to me. "Maybe there's hope for me and Christmas yet."

"I know it sounds corny, but there really is magic in the air this time of year. Sometimes you just have to look a little harder, but it is there."

Holly stares at me for a moment before bursting out laughing. "You are such a cheeseball." Scooting closer, she straddles me, sitting on my lap. "But I think I'll keep you."

"Yeah?" I brush my nose along the slope of her neck. "What are you going to do with me?" I suck lightly until I elicit the moan that I crave from her.

"How tied to your afternoon plans are you? Because I've got to say, I'd happily spend the rest of Hollymas right here."

I'm about to assure her that can be arranged when her phone buzzes from her purse.

"I should get that, Mom said she might need some help cooking tonight." She grabs her purse from where she dropped it by the roller door and settles back next to me. Scanning the screen, her brows pull together.

"She need you?"

"No, it's Brandon." She hands me the phone to read his messages.

Having car trouble, so won't be home until tomorrow.

We're going to go straight to Mom & Dad's for the party.

Stay at ours another night, you can keep Nick company.

"He probably wouldn't be saying that if he knew *how* I was going to keep you company." She snickers.

A fleeting feeling of guilt hits me, but it's quickly replaced with relief at not having to come clean for another day.

"So, we have an extra twenty-four hours, however will we spend them?"

"I can think of a few ways," she breathes. "On your back, O'Connor, I owe you a thank you."

"Yes, ma'am."

❦

I stroll through the Curtis house, enjoying the atmosphere and keeping a lookout for Holly.

We both moved back to our apartments earlier this afternoon, after agreeing not to talk to Brandon until the day after Christmas. It's going to be hard pretending that there's nothing going on between us tonight, but we decided that this party wasn't the right time.

I'd hate to break any of the Curtises' valuables when Brandon kicks my ass.

Seeing a flash of long, wavy brown hair and a bare shoulder that I instantly recognize as belonging to Holly, I follow her through to the empty outdoor deck.

She startles when I grab her from behind and place a kiss just under her ear.

"Are you following me, creeper?"

"Always," I murmur against her skin. *Peppermint.*

"Weirdo." She slaps my hands away and then motions for me to follow her to the darkened corner. "Look."

I shift my gaze around, looking all around us, but see nothing. "Look at what?"

"Up there." She points to the ceiling where I notice a small bunch of mistletoe has been hung.

"So, it's not so much that I'm a creeper, more that you lured me out here to have your way with me?"

An exaggerated gasp escapes her lips and she clutches her chest. "I would never."

I raise an eyebrow at her. "Okay, I totally would, but this was a lucky coincidence. Besides, mistletoe started this whole thing, it seems appropriate we found some tonight."

I slide a hand up her neck, into her hair, and skate a thumb over her lips. "Couldn't agree more."

Dipping my head, I take her mouth in a gentle kiss that I'm about to deepen when a noise at the back door has us breaking apart.

"Nick, you out here?"

Brandon's voice shocks me out of whatever spell Holly has me under and I step out of the shadows, closely followed by Holly.

"What are you two doing?" His eyes are narrowed suspiciously. Luckily Holly is faster on her feet than I am.

"There was a spider, Nick was just killing it."

Brandon rolls his eyes and teases her before she makes an excuse and leaves us alone, mouthing "Sorry" to me behind his back.

"Here." Brandon thrusts a beer at me and makes his way over to the chairs on the other side of the deck. I follow and take a seat next to him.

"You guys just get back?" I hadn't seen him when I did a lap of the house.

"Yeah, not long ago. You back in your apartment?"

"Moved back today. I should get the name of the plumber for you, they left the bathroom looking better than before they were there."

"Huh. That's good."

"You okay?" I run a hand through my hair nervously. "You seem distracted."

He laughs. "Yeah, I'm good, man. Really good." He takes a slug of his beer and looks at me. "Amy's pregnant."

"Shit, that's... that's amazing. Congratulations." I tap my bottle against his.

"She wanted to tell her folks first, so that's what we were doing this week. We're telling Mom, Dad, and Holly tonight after the party, but I wanted to tell you first." He shifts in his seat, so he's facing me. "You're like my brother, Nick. I know I don't do the emotional shit often, but I'm glad you moved in next door all those years ago. I'm glad you got your shit together—

I'm *proud* of you for getting your shit together—and mostly I'm glad you're going to be around to watch my kid grow up."

He claps me on the back and stands up. "It's fucking freezing out here, I'm heading back inside. Listen, don't mention the baby to anyone, okay? Not even Amy. She wants to be at every announcement and she'll kill me if she finds out I told you without her." He runs a critical eye over me. "You okay?"

"Yeah," I choke out. "You go inside, I'll find you, I just want to finish my drink out here."

He shrugs and heads in, leaving me alone.

What the fuck am I doing?

Brandon has been like my brother since we were eight years old. Mr. and Mrs. Curtis have opened their home to me and treated me like a third child. And I repay that by fucking their daughter and sister?

Not fucking. You love her, asshole.

But does that matter? If I really love her, would I let her risk her relationship with her brother? She's going to be an auntie, for Christ's sake.

I might be prepared to risk my relationship with Brandon, but what sort of asshole would I be to risk hers?

13

HOLLY

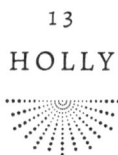

"Thanks for looking after the house while we were gone." Amy wraps me up in a warm hug. I swear my sister-in-law gives the best hugs. "I hope it wasn't too weird with Nick there."

"No, it was fine. It was kind of nice spending some time with him."

"Was it? Huh." She nods her head thoughtfully.

"What?"

"No, nothing," she exclaims. "I thought it might be —" Our across-the-street-neighbor calls her name, cutting her off. "Shit, I'm sorry, I need to talk to her for a second. I'll be back, okay?"

Nodding, I head for the kitchen feeling a bit peckish. I am almost there when a hand grabs me from behind, yanking me into the formal dining room, that has been closed off to guests.

"Nick! What the hell," I demand before noticing how shaken he looks. "What's wrong?"

He pulls me into a hug, wrapping his arms around me in the way I have come to love. Making me feel safe.

Making me feel *loved*.

He shatters that security in an instant.

"I think we've made a mistake, Hols."

I think we've made a mistake, Hols.

"What?" I push him away and step back until I hit the table. "What the hell do you mean, you think we've made a mistake?" The words sting my tongue as I force them out.

"This could ruin everything, Holly. Nothing will ever be the same if we do this. No matter what, it all changes."

"You chickenshit." I shake my head in disbelief. "We have been talking about this all along. Telling him was always the plan and now you decide you're scared of losing your little buddy?" I can't stop my sneer, the pain of rejection making me cruel.

"You want to pretend it was a mistake? Blame it on the mistletoe?" I yell. "Is that what you want?"

"No. Jesus." He pulls out a chair and slumps down onto it. "I want you."

I can barely hear him over the noise outside this room, so I move to sit beside him.

He reaches over and drags my chair until it's right beside his. Cupping my face, he brings his forehead to mine. "I want you. I love *you*."

Now? He tells me he loves me *now*?

"Then what the *fuck* are you doing?" I ask, quietly.

"I got spooked."

I start to pull away, but he stops me.

"No, hear me out. You guys have been my second family for as long as I can remember. Talking to Brandon made me realize that I don't want to lose that. I thought I was being noble or some bullshit. Thought I was doing it for you, but it was me. The second we tell him, I could lose something that is important to me."

"Do you really think he's going to be that angry?"

"I would be, if it was my sister."

"Yes, but Brandon is a much better person than you."

He pulls away laughing.

"One hundred percent true. But he warned me off once, and he was serious."

"Then fuck Brandon, because he should know better than to involve himself in my business."

"He just wants the best for you, Holly."

"I get to decide what's best for me. Not Brandon. Not you. *Me*. Do you understand?"

"Okay." He kneads the back of his neck and stands. "We should get back out there before someone notices we're missing."

"Just a second. We're not done yet."

"Really?" He tugs on his collar uncomfortably. "I was kind of hoping that was it."

"Sit your ass down, O'Connor."

"So fucking bossy," he mutters under his breath, smirking at me and taking a seat.

"I need to know you're in this, Nick." I swallow hard, already nervous about his response. "It's got nothing to do with my brother or my parents. It's about us. Because I... I love you, too, but if you're going to get *'spooked'*." I roll my eyes. "Every time something tough comes up, then we can't do this. I won't put myself through that. Not even for you."

The room is silent and dread settles deep in my stomach. I'm about to get up and walk out, taking his silence for my answer, when he suddenly stands and pulls me up with him.

Wrapping his arms around me, he holds me close. "I solemnly swear I will never get spooked again."

I meet his eyes and allow myself to drown in their sincerity for a moment. I let myself trust in the magic he's shown me.

Let myself trust in him.

"Good enough," I whisper right before our mouths meet and I melt into the comfort of his taste.

"I knew it! I fucking *knew* it!"

Nick and I jump apart and find Brandon and Amy standing in the doorway.

Nick leans down and mumbles in my ear. "Okay, I'm a little spooked."

"Brandon, what are you doing?" I decide offense is going to be my best defense right now.

He ignores me, instead turning to his wife. "You owe me fifty bucks, Ames."

"I can't believe that stupid plan worked," she grumbles.

"Wait, what is going on right now?" I'm so confused.

"I bet Amy fifty bucks I could finally get you two together before Christmas."

I feel Nick's chest rumble at my back. "You bet Amy you could—what?"

"You heard me. I can't believe you two weren't going to tell me. It cost me five hundred bucks to get your super to agree to lie to you about the plumbing and you were going to let me go on thinking my plan had failed."

"You bribed my super—"

"You know what? Bribe is such an ugly word, Nick. I gave him a financial incentive to help nudge the course of true love." Brandon holds his hands up and looks at us innocently, while Amy shakes her head.

"Are you fucking kidding me, B?" Nick moves toward him, but I hold him back. "I've been killing myself with guilt over this and you planned the whole thing?"

The grin falls from Brandon's face and is replaced with something resembling hurt. "Well, if you had just been honest with me about this shit between you two, I wouldn't have needed to resort to these tactics."

"Brandon." I try to calm the tension between the two. "Did it occur to you to broach the subject with Nick?"

"Where's the fun in that?"

Nick groans behind me.

"How did you even know how we felt?" I can't help being curious.

"Oh, please," Amy snorts.

"Yeah, it's not like you guys were subtle. You" —he points to Nick— "have been low-key stalking her on social media for three years."

"Reeeeeally?" I turn and smile smugly at him.

"You always ask about her and every time you come

to our place, the first thing you do is go and stand in front of the mantle looking at the pictures. Specifically the pictures of Holly." He grimaces. "It's kind of creepy, dude."

I laugh, a full-on belly laugh, feeling lighter than I have all night.

"And you." Brandon turns to me. "You've had a crush on him since we were kids. I kept waiting for you to grow out of it, but you never did. Also kind of creepy, Hols."

I'm going to kill him.

"You did?" Nick's self-satisfied voice sounds behind me.

"That's neither here nor there. You—" I point a finger at Brandon. "Have far too much time on your hands."

"You guys should be thanking me."

Both Nick and I remain silent, and Brandon starts to sputter indignantly.

"You told me to stay away from her," Nick accuses, cutting Brandon off.

"Yeah, three years ago." He shrugs. "Three years ago you were a drunk asshole and I would have killed you if you touched my sister. You're not a drunk asshole anymore. Why wouldn't I want my sister with the best man I know?"

I hear Nick swallow hard behind me, but he doesn't say anything.

"C'mon, honey." Amy pulls Brandon toward the door and throws us an apologetic look over her shoulder. "Let's go get some food before I move from hungry to hangry."

"But we need to talk about the rules." He looks back at us. "I might be okay with this, but I still have ground rul—" Amy slams the door, cutting him off.

We stand there in silence, both of us still processing what just happened.

"Did you have any idea he kne—"

"Nope, not a clue. You?"

"Fuck, no." He spins me around and pulls me up flush against him. "So tell me about this crush." He smirks down at me and all I can do is shake my head, laughing.

"Nick."

"Yeah?"

"Shut up and kiss me."

He glances up at the ceiling before turning back to me. "There's no mistletoe."

"Hmm, you're right," I concede. "I guess I can wait until we find some more." I start to pull away, but he stops me.

"That would be a mistake, I think. Who knows when we'll stumble across more mistletoe?"

"What are you talking about? We know there's some out on the deck."

"Holly?"

"Hmmm?"

"Kiss me."

And I do.

EPILOGUE

HOLLY

Six months later...

"Will you please relax and just enjoy yourself."

Billie glares at me, but it loses some of its heat when you take in the floppy hat on her head and the colorful cocktail she is holding.

"That's easy for you to say, you didn't just lose your job."

I play with the straw in my own drink and consider her thoughtfully.

"You didn't lose your job, you lost your *second* job. Do you really need a second job?" I prod as tactfully as I can in making what I think is an important distinction. "I mean between working at *Avondale* and the pizzeria *and* school, you were burning yourself out."

I want to tell her I'm glad she lost the job. That I hated watching her work herself into the ground, constantly exhausted and with no real life to speak of. But I keep my mouth shut because I know my friend well enough to know all that will get me is a week of silent treatment.

"I need that money, Holly, we don't all have rich families, you know," she snipes.

I bite my tongue, knowing she's only lashing out because she's scared right now. Plus, she has a point, I have been incredibly lucky, and while my parents have always taught both Brandon and me to work hard and earn our way, I always knew I had a safe place to land if things went wrong.

Case in point, my apartment.

"At least you don't have to worry about a place to live."

She shifts uncomfortably before turning to lie on her back, flicking up sand from underneath her towel as she does.

"Yeah, about that, I need to tell you something."

"Uh huh, go ahead," I reply, already knowing I'm not going to like this.

"I know you were thinking I would sublet the apartment from you once you move in with Nick." She rolls her eyes when the giant smile I get every time moving in with Nick gets mentioned, spreads across my face. "But I just can't swing it. Even before I lost the pizzeria job, it would have been too tight." Her face is full of regret. "So, I'll be moving out when you do." She immediately pulls her hat off her head and covers her face with it, hiding away.

I look down on her from my lounge chair and try to figure out how to broach the subject I've been dreading ever since she moved in with me a year and a half ago.

"You don't need to move out."

"Yes, I do." She yanks the hat off and sits up to face me. "I can't afford the rent by myself and I've been looking, but I haven't been able to find a roommate who isn't either crazy or really, *really* crazy."

"Look, Bill, I never told you this, but Dad owns the apartment."

She looks at me and then gives a slow blink before shaking her head. "You better not be about to suggest I ask him to reduce the rent because that is not going to happen."

"No, see, the thing is, Dad doesn't charge us rent."

Confusion clouds her face. "Explain yourself."

"Look, he bought the apartment years ago. It's close to work and I love the neighborhood, so when it became vacant a couple of years ago I asked Dad if I could rent it."

"Go on," she bites out.

"He agreed, but he refused to take any money from me. I tried to insist but he wouldn't listen, so we came up with the compromise that I would make a monthly donation to a homeless shelter in exchange for living there."

Her face relaxes slightly. "Okay, I'm not entirely sure how I feel right now." She chews on her lip and then takes a large gulp of her drink. "I mean on the one hand, I'm a little pissed that I've been living rent-free in my boss's apartment for a year and a half, but I guess the shelter needs the money more than your dad, so..." She puts her drink down and leans back on her hands. "No, okay, I'm good with it. If your dad was happy for us to pay our rent money that way, then I'm fine with it. But it doesn't change things now. Even if he wanted to offer me the same deal, I can't afford that much every month, and before you say anything, no I don't want you to speak to him for me."

She closes her eyes and tilts her head up to the sun. God, she is *not* going to like this next part.

"So, here's the thing, when I found out you were looking for a place to live, I spoke to my dad about you moving in and he was all for it. He knew I was kind of lonely living by myself so he was happy for me to get a roommate. Plus, he obviously knows you and likes you and he thought we would get along well, which, you know, he was right, right? We get along really well." I'm practically pleading with her.

"Yes." She draws that one syllable out far longer than it should be.

"The only condition he had was that I didn't take any rent money from you." My body slumps as I finally spit out the words I've dreaded telling her since the day she moved in. I sense, rather than see her body tense beside me.

"But I gave you rent money every month."

"Yeah, I've just been putting it into the bank every month, I figured when one of us moved out I would give it back to you and then it wouldn't matter how mad you were." I shrug and try my best to look adorable so she can't be mad at me.

"I can't believe you!"

Hmm... guess the adorable thing didn't work.

"The water is amazing, are you guys actually going

to get in there at some point today?" Nick flops down into the chair next to mine and shakes his head in my direction, spraying me with water and causing me to squeal.

I'm about to respond when my attention is snagged by droplets inching their way down his broad chest, the sunlight highlighting his tanned skin. My eyes trace the artwork that covers his left arm and lands on the sprig of holly he recently had inked by his wrist. The permanent mark fills me with warmth and I find myself reaching out to trace a finger along it, the urge to touch him too strong to resist.

"Holly." I turn back to a red-faced Billie and my heart sinks at the anger that is rolling off her.

"Billie, it's not a big deal, really," I insist. "Dad doesn't want you to leave and he doesn't expect you to pay rent, so you can stay in the apartment. I'm sorry I wasn't exactly truthful, but it's really not a big deal."

"I don't need your charity."

"It's not charity, Bill, you're practically family."

"What's going on?" Nick's confusion is obvious.

"We're fighting Nick, Jesus, read the room." Billie turns to me with fire in her eyes. "I've already found a place and I'm moving out in two weeks. Take the cash from the bank and donate it to the shelter."

With that, she gets up and storms off toward the water.

"Do I want to know?"

"No," I sigh, slumping back into my seat. "I'll talk to her when she's calmed down. Are you ready for the move tomorrow?"

"Babe, I've been ready since the first time I asked you to move in with me, months ago." He laughs and grabs my hand, pulling me over until I land on top of him.

He's right, of course. Nick asked me to move in with him a month after the Christmas party where Brandon's deception was revealed. I, on the other hand, was trying to be sensible and not rush into anything, worried that he would get spooked again.

But after six months, I couldn't keep refusing him. Or, more specifically, I didn't want to.

"I love you." My lips find his in a kiss that is begging to be deepened.

Unfortunately for us—or fortunately, when I take a minute to remember where we are—we're interrupted by a body falling into my recently vacated chair.

"Your parents sure know how to throw a party, Holly." Tessa giggles. "Are you guys excited for the fireworks tonight? I *love* fireworks!"

My beautiful blonde friend giggles again, the first clue that she has been enjoying the open bar Mom and Dad had set up along the perimeter of our property line. Along with a buffet that I have indulged in far too much today.

So, yes, it's true to say my parents know how to throw a party and their Fourth of July barbecue is no exception.

"Enjoying that pina colada there, are ya, Tessie?" I roll over and sit up between Nick's legs.

"Mmmhmm, it's yummy," she hiccups and I feel Nick's shoulders shake with a chuckle.

"Anywho, have you seen Billie? There's someone I want to introduce her to."

I stifle a groan, knowing one of Tessa's infamous setups will only upset Billie even more. Which isn't ideal considering I want to make her forgive me before I leave tomorrow morning.

"Ooooh, never mind." I follow her gaze to the water's edge where Billie is standing alongside a giant of a man who has a face to rival any romance cover novel, with her hands on her hips.

"Who is that?" I murmur, my voice abnormally throaty, even to my own ears.

"Hey," Nick huffs in my ear.

"Love you." I twist around and brush my lips across his before turning straight back around and asking again, "Seriously, Tess, who *is* that?"

"Just a little someone I thought she should meet." She tries to wink at me, but considering she's a little 'happy' all she manages is a double blink.

"All right, big man." I run a hand along his strong thigh. "By my estimation, we have about three hours before we have to be back out here for the fireworks, which is just enough time for me to do all the filthy things to you I have planned. You ready?"

He almost knocks me off the chair in his rush to get up, but manages to save me just before my knees hit the sand.

"You two are so cute." Tessa flops back on the seat and waves us off. "Go. Go make beautiful babies that I can coo over." She tries to take a sip of her drink, but misses the straw completely.

Nick and I both freeze, her words stopping us in our tracks.

"Did you remember the condoms," I hiss.

"Yeah, they're in my suitcase."

"Oh, thank god. C'mon, let's go." I grab his hand and drag him across the beach to our childless-for-the-time-being happily ever after, never more grateful that the mistake we made under the mistletoe all those months ago has led us here.

§

Thank you so much for reading *Mistletoe Mistake*! Please consider taking a few minutes to leave a review. If you enjoyed *Mistletoe Mistake*, you'll be happy to know the series is continuing with Billie's story… You can pre-order *Miss Independent* HERE!

§

Would you like to read a *BONUS EPILOGUE* about Nick and Holly? You'll find it HERE!

§

Be sure to keep reading for an excerpt from my book *Under the Cherry Blossoms*, book one in the *Finding Forever* Series!

SNEAK PEEK: Under the Cherry Blossoms by Amali Rose

PROLOGUE

2 *003*

My head feels foggy as I watch my father from my cross-legged position on the floor where I'm sitting, still trying to make sense of everything that has happened tonight.

"Skylah?"

I blink once. Twice.

"Skylah." My father's voice is louder, more insistent this time, and I see him crouched down in front of me. He's holding my hands in his, but I can't seem to feel them. The sense of security that normally follows his touch has vanished.

"Honey, this is for the best, you'll see. Your mom and I have been so unhappy. We need this."

As the words leave his mouth I hear a glass smash on the tiled floor, just outside the bedroom door, and hear my mother's footsteps fade away as she rushes down the hall.

Sighing, my father stands up, his broad shoulders slightly hunched, and a look of frustration crosses his face. Closing his eyes, he takes a breath and seems to regroup as the sound of his phone buzzing with a text fills the air.

Looking down and pulling up the message, a slow smile lights his face, all sense of frustration gone.

It's her, I realize with horror and I feel a single tear escape. Brushing it away furiously before he can notice, I watch as he slides his phone in his back pocket and resumes packing with a renewed vigour.

Moments later, he zips his suitcase closed and approaches me.

"C'mon, honey, walk me out," Dad says, holding his hand out to me. I take it hesitantly. There's no way I can stop this so refusing seems petty, and I allow him to lead me to the front door.

"I'll call when I get home, okay?"

Home. This is your home, I want to scream. Here with me and Mom! But I don't. I nod mutely and let him draw me into a tight hug. All too soon, he pulls away and with a last brush of his hand across my cheek, he turns and walks out the door. I watch him make his way down the front path, hop into his car, gun the engine and drive off down the street. The hand I had raised to wave goodbye, drops quickly back down to my side. There's no point. He never looked back.

CHAPTER 1

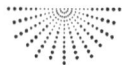

"Ugh, shit." The words fall from my lips as I trip over the cushion left on the floor with all the grace of a stumbling hippopotamus. Okay, maybe that last glass of wine wasn't the smartest idea I've ever had. As I pull myself up I search for my kindle and sigh in relief as I spot it safe on the couch. I reach down and pick it up as I make my way to my bedroom, ready to curl up and enjoy my latest book boyfriend and this wine buzz I have going on.

After getting ready for bed I am snug and settled, devouring the filthy words on the screen with the enthusiasm of someone who has clearly not enjoyed any sexy times in a ridiculously long while. As my eyes eat up the words, my hand unconsciously smooths its way down my body, seeking relief from the tension pulsing in my core. As my fingers slide through the wetness, I groan softly. Grazing my clit lightly, a shiver escapes me. I am so worked up it's only a matter of minutes before my teasing fingertips have worked their magic and I am moaning my release.

I sigh as I roll over thinking how too many of my nights are ending this way. I've almost forgotten what it feels like to have an actual guy touch me, and frankly, I'm ready to give myself the "it's not you, it's me speech". I think about the advice my best friend Cassidy gave me the other day; online dating. I mean there's no shame in it these days, right? We're all busy, it's a perfectly respectable way to meet people. And it works. I've seen the testimonials and surely, they wouldn't lie. Right?

While I still retain a bit of liquid courage, courtesy of all the wine I drank tonight, I grab my phone and google "most successful dating sites". It would seem Happily Ever After is the site of choice for all the despera... I mean, hopeful singles out there. I stifle a laugh at the name. I'm not looking for a happily ever after. Just a happily ever orgasm. So, before I lose my nerve I pull up the website and click on the 'create an account' button. Ten minutes later, I have completed my profile and set it loose into the online dating world. My smiling face gazes out at me from the phone screen and I can't help looking at myself with pity. A sense of dread settles in my stomach as I send out a silent prayer to the dick-pic gods. Please no delfies. Or, you know, at least make them dicks worthy of my admiration. Oh god, what have I done?

BEEEEEP.

I sigh quietly as I reach to open the microwave and pull out the dinner for one as Cassidy continues her rant in my ear. "Seriously, Skye, I'm not sure how much longer I can stay there. The work is boring as fuck and the people are even worse! How can I be expected to work under those conditions? I'm not getting any sleep at night because I'm falling asleep out of boredom every day!"

I try to hold in a giggle as I listen to Cassidy complain about her job in office administration. Unfortunately, the result is an unattractive snort-giggle that alerts her to my mirth. "Well, I'm glad you find my pain so funny, loser!" she shrieks, and I can feel her glowering through the phone, which causes me to lose any pretence and I burst out laughing.

"It's work, Cass, it's not supposed to be fun. It's just the eight hours we have to get through every day to get to the fun stuff."

"Speaking of the fun stuff, you wanna go out tonight? Cocktails and tapas?" The change in Cassidy's voice is immediate and if I didn't know her so well, would be slightly disconcerting. But after ten years of friendship I am used to her swift mood changes and at times like this, I am grateful for them. Her work diatribes are becoming a daily occurrence.

"I would but I've got myself a hot date tonight. Ben and I agreed to chat at 8 o'clock." I listen as Cassidy whoops loudly on the other end of the phone, mumbles something about sexting and starts to sing "bow chika wow wow."

I roll my eyes at her outburst but I can't help the smile that spreads across my face. Cass is my opposite in every way. The yin to my yang, the Scary Spice to my Baby Spice. She is the dark to my light and I couldn't imagine my life without her. She has also seen me despair over the long list of less than desirable men that have replied to my online profile, and encouraged me to persevere. Cassidy claimed the answer to my sex drought was only a click away, and don't think she didn't proclaim her triumph loudly when Ben Mackinnon appeared in my Happily Ever After mailbox. Sexy as hell and, if his messages are anything to go by, sweet, smart and funny; he ticked all my boxes and then some. And I'm not going to lie; the fact that he didn't send me a dick pic within the first ten minutes had definitely worked in his favor.

"Okay, okay, okay, enough!" I laugh as I cut Cassidy off mid-chika. "I have fifteen minutes to scarf down this meal before it's B-time so I've got to go. I'll talk to you tomorrow, okay?"

"B-time? Really? I sincerely worry about your cool cred sometimes, you nerd. But that's a topic for another day. Later, Skyballs, and remember, two hands on your phone at all times, young lady!"

I groan as Cassidy hangs up on me and I place my phone on the kitchen counter. Tucking a strand of my long brown hair behind my ear, I pick up my fork and dig into my lean cuisine. After a quick glance at the clock I see it's ten minutes to eight, and feel the butterflies start. Truth be told, I'm completely out of practice with this whole dating thing. My list of exes did nothing to change my mind and convince me that a happily ever after was in my future, and I had forgotten about this complex mix of excitement and fear which left you unsure if you were giddy or nauseous!

Placing my dishes in the dishwasher, I move to the couch and settle in for what I hope will be a long chat. Because chatting to Ben has become the highlight of my day, and while I probably should, I feel absolutely no shame in admitting that. The last month talking to him has been fun and easy; I find myself almost craving the contact with him. He has tried to convince me to meet him in person a handful of times but I've resisted. There is safety in where we are now, in the protection that the phone screen affords me. I started this online thing to find someone to have fun with. Someone who can scratch my metaphorical itch anytime it tingles, but the longer I talk to Ben, the more I can see myself falling for him and I can't let that happen. My head understands this but as my phone dings and my heart begins to pound, it's clear that my heart might not be on the same page. Ugh, someone needs to give me a stern talking to. I am a twenty-eight-year-old grown woman, not a giddy, giggling preteen. Then again, I haven't gotten laid in a while so I give myself a pass.

BEN: You there, beautiful?
  SKYE: Yep. How was your day?

Riveting, I know. Have I mentioned I'm out of practice?

. . .

BEN: Good, busy. One of the systems crashed so we spent the day trying to clean up that shit storm. I hope yours was better?

SKYE: I'm not even going to pretend to understand the computer stuff lol but it sounds like a rough day, so I'm sorry. I almost feel bad telling you that I had a fantastic day, I got a promotion!

As happy as I was about the promotion, it was bittersweet. My boss, Juliet, had informed me that she wanted to take a step back from running Books & Beans, the bookstore slash coffee shop that she owned. So, she was promoting me to manager, and while I was incredibly excited about the chance to have more responsibility, and my mind was bursting with ideas, I was also slightly terrified at the prospect of failing.

BEN: That's incredible news! We have to celebrate. What about dinner on Friday night?

My hand freezes over the phone keyboard. I'm not ready for this, it's too soon. I mean, I know that realistically it stopped being too soon about two weeks ago (according to Cassidy "Bow Chika Wow Wow" Jensen, anyway) but I'm not sure I'm ready to take that next step yet. My phone vibrates in my hand, bringing my gaze back to the screen.

BEN: Baby, I'm sorry, I have to go, work just called and they need me back there. I'll make some reservations for Friday and get back to you, okay? I'm really happy for you.

Well shit. I guess I'm meeting Ben.

Under the Cherry Blossoms is AVAILABLE NOW!

Stay Connected

Private Facebook Group: https://www.facebook.com/groups/amalisrisqueromantics
Instagram: https://www.instagram.com/authoramalirose
BookBub: https://www.bookbub.com/authors/amali-rose
Amazon: https://www.amazon.com/author/amalirose
Facebook: https://www.facebook.com/authoramalirose
Goodreads: https://www.goodreads.com/author/show/17064277.Amali_Rose

My newsletter is the best way to stay in contact with me! You'll get first look at titles, covers and release dates, plus exclusive sneak peeks!
Sign up here: https://tinyurl.com/y6h3hw9s

More by Amali Rose

Finding Forever Series
(Standalone series)

Under the Cherry Blossoms >> Fling to Forever
Romance
Dandelion Dreams >> Enemies to Lovers/Office
Romance
Amongst the Wildflowers >> Friends to Lovers
Romance
Breathing Wisteria >> Second Chance Romance
Finding Forever >> The Complete Series

Greetings From Avondale Series (Standalone Series)

Mistletoe Mistake >> Brother's Best Friend/Holiday
Romance
Miss Independent >> Billionaire Romance

Standalones:

Dating the DILF >> Single Dad Romantic Comedy

ACKNOWLEDGMENTS

As always, to every blogger who has ever read, reviewed, shared or supported me in any way, you have my complete gratitude and I will never take it for granted. *Thank you, thank you, thank you!!!*

To the person reading this... I have always had a deep passion for reading, so I know how the words we read claw their way into our hearts and find a home there. It stuns me every day that there are people who find joy in my words and I thank you from the bottom of my heart.

To my favourite people in the entire world! Kerry, Karen, Renee, Kim, Antonette, Rachel, Joz & Harper. I love you!

To every one of my friends, family and loved ones, who support me and cheer me on, you make me brave and I adore you all for it.

Writing a book can be a very solitary experience, but *publishing* a book takes a whole team. If you're lucky, you find a group of people who care about your story as much as you do. *I have been so. Incredibly. Lucky.*

Ellie McLove & Rosa Sharon (My Brother's Editor), thank you both for putting up with my inability to meet a deadline or learn where to put a damn comma. Please don't ever leave me!

Ben Ellis (Tall Story Designs), working with you is a joy! Thank you for putting up with my ramblings and somehow turning them into a work of art. My books are made better by your remarkable covers.

Kylie McDermott, Jo Webb & Alicia Mackey (Give Me Books), you are the most amazing PR team! Your kindness is equal only to your professionalism and I hope we work together on many, *many* future projects!

Last, but certainly not least, my street team! Antonette Santillo, Cassy Kubehl, Devon Farrow, Heather Poll, Katrina Haynes, Kristi Smith, Lauren Harwood, Rachel McLean, Tamara Harrington & Tre Talbot. What would I do without you?! Thank you for your constant hard work, support and encouragement. I'm keeping you all forever!!!

Huge love & hugs!
Amali xox

ABOUT THE AUTHOR

USA Today Bestselling author Amali Rose is a former blogger from Australia, who released her debut novella in 2017.

A self confessed bookworm, her love affair with the written word began as a child, with *The Magic Faraway Tree*. Her tastes have grown and evolved over the years and, after stumbling into the indie community a few years ago, she discovered her passion for romance with a side of smut.

When not reading or writing, Amali enjoys cheesy pop music, netflix marathons, and she believes strongly that pink, puppies and chocolate make the world a better place!

www.ingramcontent.com/pod-product-compliance
Lightning Source LLC
Chambersburg PA
CBHW020640130726
47903CB00003BA/932